The Katy Moon Chronicles:

Dark Dances

by Julie D. Lambert

Copyright © 2000 by Julie D. Lambert.
All rights reserved.

ISBN 0-9687719-0-4

Published by Julie D. Lambert
3629a, rue St-Denis
Montréal (Québec) H2X 3L6
Canada

Photo credits:

Bronze sculptures by Julie D. Lambert

Earth's moon photographed by Apollo 11, supplied courtesy of National Space Science Data Center

Photographs of Ms. Lambert and her sculptures by Gilles Tanguay,
with the exception of the photograph of
"New Shoes" on wooden base
which was supplied courtesy of
Galerie Diagram-Art.

Cover Montage by David H. M. Lambert

For the men in my life:

David, James, and Gilles

Acknowledgements

No book sees the light of day without interrupting the lives of a whole boatload of innocent bystanders. My most heartfelt thanks to my friends and family who helped so cheerfully including most particularly

...the Sistahs: O-dahlin', La Belle Susan, and Her Serene Highness Queen Jeanieweanie, for their intelligent criticisms and endless hand-holding....

...Charles and David for saving me from the Internet...

...and most of all Gilles, my patient and sensitive editor, my spiritual partner, and the other (smarter) half of my brain. J'ai commencé à cause de moi, mais j'ai fini à cause de toi. Un gros merci. Je t'aime énormément...

-JDL

Author's Note
(About the dance terms)

You can't write a cookbook without using terms like "mince" and "sauté." It's almost as impossible to write about dancers without using technical dance terminology. I've tried to keep the jargon to a minimum, but there are instances where it just doesn't read right without it. So for my readers who just can't stand it if they don't understand every word, a brief glossary is included at the back of the book.

Prologue:

Adagio by Candlelight

Half-hidden behind twelve ancient water elms, the elaborately gingerbreaded old Victorian house crouched like a bejeweled troll. It was an eccentricity of its owner that no electric lights had ever been installed in it, although it was equipped with many state-of-the-art electronics. Tonight, as on most nights, only two of its many rooms showed candlelight through their windows and could be seen dimly from across the small private lake that lay beyond the trees.

On the first floor a man sat at a heavily carved walnut desk in the library, making lists and taking notes as he prepared for the complex work that would occupy the next several months of his life. The room was bright with dozens of tiny candle flames, the white wax tapers various heights and thicknesses, in all manner of silver candelabra and candlesticks. It was too early in the fall for the fire in the hearth that would add to the room's illumination in deep winter, but the many mirrors reflected and multiplied the individual candle flames until they seemed to number in the hundreds.

The man leaned back in his chair, frowning and drumming his fingers on the arm of his chair. He was uncomfortably restless in spite of the lateness of the hour. He reached for the old-fashioned bell-pull which hung behind him on the wall, hesitated, then pulled its tasseled cord.

On the fourth floor, a single candle flickered in a small bed-sitting room where a dancer sat still and pale in a gilded chair, her dark green eyes expressing nothing, waiting. She lifted her eyes to the small bell in her room as it rang. She stood up, took her single candle, and descended the long staircase.

From outside the house her candle could be seen appearing and disappearing in the window at each landing as she walked downward, leaving the house dark behind her.

She wore a long black velvet cape that reached from her neck to the floor. When she reached the library, she stopped in the doorway, and in the candlelight the black velvet seemed to disappear, giving the illusion of only a beautiful pale face floating in the dark accompanied by two delicate hands. Her dark hair merged with the blackness behind her, and outside the warm circle of her face and hands, the entire world seemed dark.

The man did not speak to her; he had not found it necessary to speak to her in perhaps five years. He picked up the largest of the candelabra and walked past her to the entryway of the house, then up the broad staircase. She followed him silently.

On the second floor they entered what had at one time been a ballroom, now fitted at one end with a small curtained stage. The audience area contained a single chair in which the man seated himself, shifting impatiently in the chair as the woman mounted the steps beside the stage and disappeared behind the curtain. It always took more time than he liked for her to light the footlight candles and the big candelabra that hung over the stage.

When she had finished, she pressed the mechanism that would raise the curtain after a five second delay, allowing her to take her place in the center of the stage.

As the curtain rose, the slow, melancholy strains of Albinoni's "Adagio in G Minor" filled the room, and she began to dance.

The man watched avidly, seeming to try to drink something--some sustenance--out of the sight of her as she moved.

She began by using the long cloak, dragging it to describe slow circles on the floor as she turned. Gradually she rose on pointe, and the hem lifted slightly off the floor as well, billowing like a hoop skirt as she turned faster.

She released the clasp on the front and held the long velvet behind her now, making larger and larger circular shapes with it. Under the cape she wore a long-sleeved black velvet unitard so that her body still seemed almost invisible, black against black against black. Tiny lines of black crystal beads made her arms and legs and torso appear as pure movement in empty space.

Turn melted into turn, then paused like a softly drawn breath. One leg drifted lazily upward as though it were lighter than the surrounding air and required her attention to remain in contact with the earth. Her supporting foot rose to half-pointe, then to full pointe, where she hovered for an impossibly long moment...

The man watched hungrily. After a few moments, he leaned forward in his seat, his face growing darker, desperate. Slowly, almost imperceptibly slowly, he moved forward, a malevolent tide rising toward the dancer until he stood at the very edge of the stage, grasping its edge in angry panic, his whole body shaking.

Suddenly he lifted both fists above his head and brought them down on the wooden stage with all his force, making it reverberate and echo like a timpani. The woman stopped and stood still, her breath coming from her in gasps.

Without a word he spun on his heel and swept from the ballroom, the music washing away from him like the wake of a passing ship as he surged through it.

She stood still, waiting until the music finished in case he returned, though she knew he would not.

Then she carefully extinguished all the candles except her one, wrapped herself again in the long velvet cape, and climbed the long staircase to her room where she sat again in her gilded chair. To wait.

The man raged back to his library and leaned against the Italian marble mantelpiece, shaking and weeping. He reached out an arm and swept it viciously across the mantle, sending a priceless collection of jeweled porcelain eggs to the floor where they shattered. Then he picked up a small antique table and smashed it against the wall until it lay splintered beyond recognition.

In her bed-sitting room, the woman felt the house shudder as the front door slammed, but her perfect face did not change expression, and she did not go to the window to watch him storm down to the lake.

At the water's edge he waded in until he stood hip deep in the dark water. The long, thick-bladed grasses that grew beneath the surface moved like sinuous snakes around his legs. The cold water calmed him somewhat, and he stared upward at the night sky.

Finally he spoke despairingly to the moon, to the night, to the stillness around him. "She is empty. I can get nothing more from her. She is starving me. I must have another before the year turns."

Behind him, in the window of the bed-sitting room, the dancer sat in her gilded chair and waited.

Part One:

The Chosen

Chapter 1:

Today. It's Today.

Before dawn in an affluent suburban neighborhood, Katy Moon made soft, panicky, whimpering sounds in her sleep. After several attempts, the cry broke at last out of her paralyzed throat. And woke her up.

The big two-story house on Wisteria Street was still and silent. Her heart was pounding, and real tears were in her eyes, but gradually she recognized the darkness around her as only the familiar darkness of her room. She had left behind in her dream whatever had terrified her.

Scraps of her nightmare re-played themselves in her head. She had been on-stage with a lot of other dancers, wandering in urgent confusion, not knowing her place... A voice from above her had called out the names of dance steps, but she hadn't recognized any of the French terms--the sounds didn't have any meaning attached to them... She was standing in a spotlight, everyone was watching her, waiting for her to do something, and she couldn't figure out what...

The rest was just a thin spectral cord of fear stretching between Katy and the dream, tying her to it. One thought severed the cord, circling furiously around her brain: "*Today. It's today.*"

She sat up, irritating Nijinska, the calico cat sleeping warmly beside her, who was suddenly turned upside down in an earthquake of sheets and eyelet lace covers. The elderly cat protested loudly.

"Sorry, Nij," Katy said as she switched on a lamp. "Go back to sleep. I'm getting up."

Katy shook her head a couple of times, trying to clear the remnants of her nightmare, planted her bare feet on the coolness of her hardwood floor, and headed for the bathroom.

Nijinska blinked in the unwelcome light and considered her options. Yes, she could go back to sleep. The covers were still warm. There was no chance of breakfast for another hour. But there was a feeling in the air, a smell of significance with a hint of some change, some possibility. And just underneath it a darker smell... some danger. She got up.

Nijinska and Katy (whom the cat always thought of as the cat-language equivalent of "Moon-child") were exactly the same age, born in fact on the same exact day. But a cat is old at age 13, whereas a human girl is not at all, and Nijinska had always felt that this accelerated maturity carried with it a certain responsibility.

Katy herself now felt only the fluttery stomach she always felt before an audition. What she did today would put her on one of three lists: "Fair," "The Best", or "Hopeless," and she wasn't at all sure which list she belonged on.

The feeling was somewhere between waking up Christmas morning and sick-at-your-stomach-falling-down-a-well fear, but it was different from the helplessness of the dream. Here, in the real world, she *knew* what all the French terms meant.

The adrenaline was already so strong that she didn't even turn on the radio as she usually did when she first woke up. Between the bed and the bathroom, as she rubbed the sleep out of her eyes, she bumped into the same blue chair she always bumped into.

It was a popular sport among the other eighth graders to bet on how many pieces of furniture Katy would hit as she walked through a room. After ten years of hearing ballet teachers shout, "Don't look at the floor," now she didn't. The habit was a virtue on a stage, a handicap in a normal room filled with sharp-cornered furniture.

Nijinska padded silently after her, watching apprehensively as Katy absently rubbed her often-bruised hip and turned on the shower.

The sting of the shower and the mingled scents of soap and shampoo were keenly real, and Katy stood breathing the scented steam and feeling the warm soapy waterfalls as they ran through her hair and down her body until the last shreds of the dream washed down the drain.

"What?" Katy asked the cat who was still sitting and watching the girl cautiously as she emerged from the shower and wrapped herself in a big towel.

Nijinska stood up and took a step forward until she could touch Moon-child's bare, wet foot with one paw to express her concern.

"It was just a dream. I'm fine," Katy said. "I don't know what you're so worried about. It's an audition, and I'm a little nervous, okay? That's normal."

Nijinska squinted skeptically.

Katy dug down into the back of a dresser drawer, raking through its contents until she found the new pair of pink tights she had been hoarding unopened just for this audition. Leaving the drawer open with a half-dozen pairs of faded old tights dangling over its front edge, she sat on the bed and slid the new ones out of their cellophane envelope, still folded in a crisp crease around a cardboard rectangle. They were the expensive kind with seams up the back to make her long legs look even longer, hard to find in her small size; their brand-new softness made her smile slightly.

Her legs were still damp from the shower, but she worked the tights on, hopping a little as she pulled them over her hips. She meticulously straightened the seams, checking them several times in the mirror while Nijinska stood by the bedroom door and watched.

Katy deliberated carefully over which black leotard to wear, and tried three of them on. To a non-dancer, all black leotards are pretty much the same. Some even believe that there are no such things as fat mirrors and thin mirrors. Katy knew better, and she left the camisole and the short-sleeved ones in little wads on the floor. The long-sleeved one with the low back made her look thinnest. Katy Moon was no fool.

Her long honey-blond hair wasn't quite dry yet, but it was going straight into a bun anyway. She combed it carefully into a perfect ponytail, twisted the heavy tail, wrapped it around and around itself, and nailed it into place with a fistful of extra-long hair pins. She shook her head to make sure it felt solid, then applied a layer of gel and most of a can of hairspray, sending Nijinska scurrying under the bed in fear for her lungs. Her hair was now a smooth, sleek, streaky-blond helmet that would hold up in a hurricane.

Finishing touches were easy: no jewelry, no colored nail polish. She was lucky enough to have thick, dark eyelashes that needed no mascara to accent her blue-gray eyes; it might run when she sweat, and her mother wouldn't allow it anyway.

She tried, as she did every morning, to stick down the strange, upturned corners of her eyebrows. She hated them and thought they made her look like Spock on the old Star Trek series. She got them from her father, whose eyebrows did the same thing. He called her Elf because of them, and she liked that, but she still hated the eyebrows themselves. Every morning she pasted them down with a little Vaseline. And every morning an hour later they had sprung back up to point skyward.

After the eyebrow ritual, there was just a little natural-looking lipstick, a soft spray of cologne, and one individual touch: a small cluster of pink silk flowers anchored firmly to the side of her bun--pretty, classical, and not too outlandish. Nothing that said "trouble-maker," but enough so that the judges at the audition could say to each other, "And for the part of Clara? I liked Katy Moon. Oh, you remember--the girl with the pink flowers in her hair."

In a room with 100 bun-headed clones in black and pink, you had to give them something to describe you with.

Looking critically at the effect in the mirror, she was reasonably satisfied. Except of course for the usual list of complaints and delusions: that her long neck was too short, that her delicate ankles were too knobby, and that her board-flat stomach looked "poochy" to her even in her thinnest leotard. Katy had mastered one of the early lessons of a ballet dancer: identify all real flaws in the mirror, then invent a half-dozen extras.

"Maybe they'll let us wear skirts," she muttered, tying a small wispy chiffon wrap around her tiny hips hopefully. "As if!"

The skirt came off with a jerk, but she tossed it into her dance bag just in case. She checked her shoes: two pairs of pink ballet slippers in case of a blow-out, character shoes, and her pointe shoes. The audition wouldn't be on pointe; the girls in Katy's age group hadn't been working on pointe long enough for their laborious stumblings to qualify as dancing. But she always took her pointe shoes with her anyway. They were pink satin credentials. The proof of who she was. Like a driver's license for dance.

Katy heard a quick knock on her door, followed by her mother's voice. "Katy? You up? Six forty-five. Leave in an hour."

Rebecca Moon was a no-nonsense mother. A marvel of efficiency, grooming, and uncompromising dedication to her children's success, she was not the sort of mother who wanted you in her lap very often (unless someone was in the room with a camera), but she was one hundred percent reliable when you had to get somewhere on time.

"Yes ma'am. I'm dressed."

Rebecca opened the door and stuck her head in. "What do you want for breakfast?"

"I'm not hungry." Katy had no hope of being able to choke down breakfast.

"Katy, you can't take a three-hour audition with nothing in your stomach." Her mother's limited capacity for sympathy did not extend to nonsense like nervous stomachs.

"I'll take some yogurt and trailmix with me. I can eat at the break."

"Katy!"

"Mom, I promise you, if I try to eat right now I'll throw up."

Rebecca sighed an irritated little sigh, but she withdrew and closed the door.

Katy had a feeling that the breakfast discussion was not over, but meanwhile she had an hour to stretch. She sat on the floor, her legs straight out to the sides in second position, and leaned forward with her back straight until she could put her elbows on the floor and rest her chin in her hands. No need to push it. She had plenty of time.

Nijinska took up her usual position facing Moon-child, looking earnestly up into her face. The two of them stared at each other a long time, the cat concerned, the girl reassuring. They understood each other precisely.

Katy didn't yet realize that not everyone did this with their cats. It was a subtle thing, not as though they discussed politics or traded recipes for seafood dishes. They were just keenly attuned to each other's emotions in a primitive, non-verbal way. Nijinska felt that it was a bit unusual (since no one else could do it with her), but she had no words for explaining that to Moon-child.

Katy worked slowly and systematically through her series of splits and stretches, holding each position until she could feel the muscle relax and lengthen. She was trying a new stretch that she had seen another dancer doing in the studio dressing room: stand in a doorway, put the arch of your supporting foot against the doorjamb, hold onto the door frame with both hands, slide the working leg up the door frame pulling your body forward until you're in a vertical split with one leg over your head and your nose on your knee. As she got into position and was holding the stretch, her bedroom door slowly swung open.

Katy frowned at the interruption, then laughed. It was her four-year-old sister Abigail, clutching a breakfast plate of toast, bacon, and eggs. It was tipped at such an angle that the contents would have been left on the floor except for the fact that the toast had wedged itself against one chubby hand and formed a blockade holding the eggs (mostly) on the plate. Behind her was Alexis, Abigail's identical twin, carrying what was left of a glass of orange juice.

Both of them had stopped stone-still, jaws dropped in amazement at Katy's position. They looked exactly as they would have looked if they had walked in and seen a pink rhinoceros sitting on the bed.

As usual, Alix spoke for both of them. "Wow!" she whispered. "Does dat hurt?"

"No," said Katy.   "But I don't want an audience right now, guys. And I don't want breakfast."

The two little red-heads remained silently frozen to the spot, watching with wider and wider eyes as Katy changed legs and repeated the stretch with the other leg.

"Go!"   Katy commanded in her most authoritative big-sister voice, which as usual had no effect except to make Alix get that hard "you're not the boss of me" set to her mouth.

"Mama says you're 'posed to eat it," Alexis said, firmly in the right and knowing it. Abigail stood with her mouth still open, staring at Katy.

Katy knew when she was out-gunned. "Fine. Just leave it on the dresser. And *go!*" The two little girls did, but with agonizing slowness, moving at roughly the speed of two small glaciers.

When they finally inched out the door and Katy was left alone with only Nijinska as audience, she turned to the cat and silently nodded to her to help herself to the food. In a few seconds Nijinska had carefully picked her way from the floor to the bed to the dresser (being past the age when she enjoyed big jumps) and settled into the eggs. When she finished those, she lifted the two strips of bacon delicately from the plate and carried them under the bed, stashing them away for a mid-afternoon snack.

The clock gradually ticked down to 7:30, and Katy finished her stretching by shaking out the muscles in her legs. The audition started at 9:00. They would leave the house at 7:45 and be at the studio by 8:05, plenty of time to register and still get a good place at the barre and stretch again.

Katy pulled a sweatsuit on over her leotards and tights, stepped into her sneakers, re-checked her dance bag, and headed for the car, banging into three pieces of furniture between her bedroom and the back door.

Her father waved sleepily to her from the breakfast table where he bounced a twin on each knee and tried to drink his coffee over their heads.

Her mother was already behind the wheel, her own coffee cup in hand. "Baxter College, right?" Rebecca asked as she turned the key in the ignition.

"Baxter College," Katy affirmed.

"Can I see the paper?" Rebecca held out her hand for the sheet of directions. She liked to verify details several times before proceeding, especially when the source of information was her oldest daughter.

Katy handed over the sheet, wondering if her mother would ever believe that she could correctly read "Baxter College" after the word, "Where."

She knew that the answer to that was, "Probably not." She was resigned to it, but it saddened her.

In fairness to Rebecca, it did sometimes seem that Katy had an extremely casual relationship with facts. This annoyed and worried Rebecca, who could not imagine how anyone could sit, one sock in hand, lost in a fantasy until the school bus had come and gone. Even less could she imagine bursting into hysterical sobs over a maudlin poem about a little homeless kid and his letter to Santa, as Katy had done last year.

Katy was a mystery to her, and Rebecca Moon did not trust mysteries. Particularly not with audition instructions.

"Baxter College," Rebecca read from the sheet of paper Katy handed her, "West parking lot, Jonathan Haskins Memorial Hall, front door. Got it." And she slammed the car into gear.

As they backed out of the driveway and drove off down Wisteria Street, Nijinska watched anxiously from an upstairs window. In spite of Katy's assurances and the bacon stashed under the bed, the cat was not comfortable with the feel of the day, and she patrolled the house nervously several times before curling up on the pillow where she found Moon-child's scent both comforting and disturbing, like a reminder of something she was supposed to do.

Chapter 2:

The First Doorway

The dance studio at Baxter College was the only one in town big enough to hold all the dancers who showed up for *Nutcracker* auditions. Not because the college had a great dance department--it didn't.   Most of their dance students were overweight beginners.   But dance counted as a Physical Education credit at Baxter, and the college had to build a studio the size of a gymnasium to accommodate all the young women who naively assumed that dance would require less sweating less than basketball.

As Katy and her mother pulled into the west parking lot, a group of mothers and daughters with dance bags were entering the building marked Jonathan Haskins Memorial Hall.

"There, Mom!" Katy pointed. "The Haskins building. Right there." They parked and got out.

But when Katy and her mother reached the door, it was locked. Katy peered in through the glass.

"How can it be locked?"   Rebecca Moon demanded, her sense of the predictable grievously offended. "We just saw people going in!"

"I can't see anybody in the lobby," Katy said. She tried the door again. Locked.

The two of them looked around the parking lot. Plenty of cars. No actual people.

"This is weird," Katy muttered. She tried the door again. It was just as locked as it had been five seconds ago.

Her mother tried the door again. They both put their foreheads against the glass, cupped their hands around their eyes, and squinted, trying to see something in the darkened interior. Katy's mother banged on the door with her fist and called, "Hello?!?"

No response. Katy was starting to feel a little panicked. "Mo-om?"

Her mother took the sheet of directions out of Katy's hands and compared the building and the parking lot with the written instructions. Then she double checked the date and time.

"This is ridiculous," her mother grumbled, "Jonathan Haskins Memorial Hall. West parking lot. Front door..."

She huffed in irritation and folded the instruction crisply into her purse. "Come on, Katy. We'll go around the back. There has to be a door open somewhere." She took a last sip from her mug. "I wish I had another cup of coffee," she sighed as they started down a little alley that snaked around the side of the building.

They immediately lost sight of the west parking lot behind them, so they didn't see the group of three nervous dancers and their mothers walk up to the front door of the Jonathan Haskins Memorial Hall, open it, and walk into a brightly lit lobby where thirty-two other dancers were lined up at registration tables, giggling and talking.

The twisty little alley led Katy and her mother to a series of locked side doors. The two doors at the back of the building were also locked. Between them a short flight of concrete steps led down to a basement door. Unlike the ground-floor doors, this one was not metal but wood, with faded peeling paint. It hung slightly crooked on a broken hinge and looked as though it would fall apart with the next stiff breeze.

Rebecca Moon's mouth was getting tighter and tighter, a sign Katy recognized. Her mother was about to Take Matters Into Her Own Hands. The Jonathan Haskins Memorial Hall was in big trouble.

Rebecca Moon started down the basement steps. "Come on, Katy."

"Ummm, Mom? Maybe we should check the front door again..." Katy started, although she knew it was useless. Katy did not like the look of that basement. It reminded her of something...

The basement door was sturdier than it looked, but in the end it was no match for an irate Moon-mom. The broken hinge gave way the third time Rebecca jerked on it, and suddenly they were looking into a long dark hallway, like a tunnel. A dim light shone from an open door at the far end, giving just enough light to see the dust and cobwebs floating upward in the unexpected breeze that came in behind Rebecca through the basement door.

Katy knew--she *knew*--that she didn't want to go in there. She also knew what it reminded her of now. It was her nightmare. There had been a door like this in her nightmare. With something dangerous behind it. She had braced herself against the door to hold it closed...

But Rebecca was already halfway down the dark hall/tunnel before Katy could get a word squeaked out.

Ahead of her, Katy saw her mother stop in the lighted doorway. "Thank heavens," Rebecca sighed, a look of relief spreading across her face.

"I'm trying to find the *Nutcracker* auditions, and the front door is locked. How do I get to the dance studio from here?"

Katy had caught up to her mother by now, and peered into the light. The room seemed to be a costume shop. It was cluttered with sewing machines, dressmaker's dummies, and racks of old-fashioned clothing.

Standing at the back of the room was a precious little old woman with bright blue eyes and unruly white hair wound around her head in messy braids, making her round face even rounder. She wore an absurd dress made of patches of wildly-colored silk, much too long for her, so the skirts dragged along the dusty floor behind her as she moved toward Rebecca.

"Locked? Really?" the old woman asked, making deeper wrinkles as she frowned and peered over the rims of her little circular glasses. "Odd."

"Odd," agreed Rebecca, not very patiently, "but locked nevertheless. Is there an elevator?"

"Very *odd*," the old woman re-emphasized. She seemed to be examining Rebecca's face as though it troubled her. As though she didn't understand this particular face being in this particular place.

"Or a staircase?" chimed in Katy.

Katy stood half-hidden in the dusty gloom behind her mother. As she spoke, the old woman noticed her for the first time. Her deep wrinkles slowly rearranged themselves around her round, owlish spectacles into a smile of recognition--the sort of smile you smile when you find something you've been looking for for a long time.

"Ah yes... Locked..." The old woman smiled into Katy's eyes for a moment. "So you're auditioning, are you? By the most interesting coincidence," said the old woman as she stepped around Rebecca, "I'm the costume mistress." Now she stood in front of Katy and extended her hand in solemn introduction. "Mrs. Pye. What's your name, dear?"

"Katy Moon." Mrs. Pye's hand felt dry as she shook it, and sort of crisp-thin, as old peoples' hands often do, but also soft and unusually warm. A light scent of nutmeg drifted up out of the restless folds of her skirt.

"And what part are you auditioning for, Katy Moon?"

Katy reddened a little, embarrassed at being asked to state out loud what she hoped for. "Well, last year I got Mirlitons, so this year I might be able to get 'Waltz of the Flowers.' " It was not an untrue statement--just an evasive one.

To Katy's surprise, Mrs. Pye reached out a hand made knobby by arthritis and lightly touched the corner of one of Katy's elf-like eyebrows where it turned straight up.

With a sudden flash of sickening fear, Katy was back in her dream. The door she was holding closed, the door that was keeping her safe from Something, melted like warm wax under her hands.

Behind the door was nothing. Literally nothing. Even the floor dissolved away to a dark emptiness that churned her stomach. The vast darkness was terrifying. But also... fascinating... There was something deep in it that called her. That wanted her. That loved her.

With a sickening lurch, she felt herself drop into the deep emptiness. Then came a great rush of warmth and an enfolding, as though she was no longer falling but floating upward with musty, nutmeg-scented silk patches billowing around her like wings.

Then she was back in the basement, facing this odd little owl-faced woman.

" 'Waltz of the Flowers?' " Mrs. Pye asked, still searching Katy's eyes. "Not Clara?"

Distracted and shaken by her colliding sensations, Katy was now unable to hedge her reply. "Yes," she admitted frankly, "I think I have a chance at Clara."

"Clara," murmured Mrs. Pye. The old woman seemed disturbed by the thought.

"Umm... Is this your sewing room?" asked Katy, as a diversionary tactic. "Where you make the costumes?"

"No, no... This room is..." Mrs. Pye turned around herself in a small circle, seeming to search for a clue as to what the room was and to whom it belonged.

"I'm sure it's the costume shop for the college, Katy," Rebecca put in. "Now, the stairs?"

"Quite!" exclaimed Mrs. Pye happily. "The college! Exactly! Exactly. And I came down to find something... something I forgot..." Mrs. Pye turned another small bewildered circle. "Ah! This."

She held out her hand proudly. In it was a rose-colored tape measure with strange black markings on it like Roman numerals, but not quite. It was unlike any tape measure that Katy had ever seen, and she tried to look more closely, but Mrs. Pye whisked it into a pocket of her skirt.

"Okay, we *really* need to get upstairs," insisted Rebecca.

"Oh my, of course you do, and here I stand," apologized Mrs. Pye. "Of course there's an elevator, dear. Follow me. This... Umm. No, *this* way..."

The old woman led them down a series of hallways, chattering and switching on lights as

she went, Katy and Rebecca following close
behind.   Mrs. Pye's silk patches billowed and
flowed like water around her, seeming to change
colors and designs at each step. By some miracle
of foot and fabric her skirts always swooshed out
from under her step just before she tripped on
them.

The elevator was not far, but Mrs. Pye got
turned around twice and had to retrace her steps,
shaking her head good-naturedly at her
confusion.

Nevertheless, only moments later Katy and
Rebecca were standing in the elevator, and Katy
was holding the door open, saying, "Are you going
up too, Mrs. Pye?"

"Me? Oh no, dear, not yet. I'll be up in a bit
to watch your audition. I will be holding you
tightly in my thoughts, Katy Moon," Mrs. Pye
assured her warmly, "and hoping for the very best
for you."

Strangely, it seemed to Katy that the meaning
underneath that sentence wasn't quite as clear as
the words themselves seemed to be.   But she
thanked the old woman politely.

"Gotta go, Katy," Rebecca said as she pushed
the button for the ground floor. "Thank you, Mrs.
Pye."

"Bye," Katy waved. "Nice to meet you!"

"Nice to meet you, too, dear..."

Mrs. Pye's gentle voice was fading even before
the elevator door whooshed closed, but Katy
almost thought she heard a last word that could
(oddly) have been, "...finally."

The thought was gone even before the elevator
reached the brightly lit lobby crowded with
dancers, mothers, and teachers.

"Katy, you dropped something." Rebecca picked up a sheet of paper lying on the gray carpet of the elevator.

Katy glanced at it and shook her head. "It's not mine," she said.

Rebecca sighed a long-suffering mother-sigh. "I saw it fall out of your dance bag," she corrected her absent-minded daughter. Rebecca tucked the paper back into Katy's bag as they approached the registration table.

Katy looked again at the paper. It was yellowed with age, crumbling at the edges, and filled with closely-spaced lines of spidery hand-writing. It began:

I have seen a most extraordinary child today.

While Katy stood in line to register, Rebecca complained to a uniformed facilities employee about the locked front door.

The man just stared at her blankly.

In the basement Mrs. Pye sat and hummed an odd little song, smiling to herself, making her silk patches dance. Once in a while a rose-colored butterfly with markings like Roman numerals (but not quite) would flutter up out of her lap and circle her head, landing in her white braids like an ornament. Her humming became more complex, and she seemed to hum both the melody and the harmony at the same time.

Of course, that's impossible. But the butterflies liked it.

In the house on Wisteria Street, Nijinska at last went back to sleep on Moon-child's pillow.

Chapter 3:

Number 76

"Name?" The hatchet-faced woman at the registration desk did not smile or even look up as she asked the question.

"Katy Moon." Katy's voice wobbled a little. It wasn't her first audition, but somewhere deep in the pit of her stomach she knew that she would always experience this same miserable feeling of fear and intimidation every time she walked into one. Every time. For the rest of her life.

The grim registrar ran her finger down a long list and made a check-mark as she held out her other hand. "Resumé?"

Katy handed her the crisp one-page history of her training with her photograph on the back in the required arabesque. She noticed with a twinge of embarrassment that her hand shook as she held out the paper.

With one efficient sweep, the registrar stapled the resumé to a blank form, wrote the number "76" at the top, and handed it back to Katy along with a twelve-inch square of white cloth with the same number "76" written on it in large, aggressive, Marks-a-lot numbers.

"Fill out the form. Leave it on the table at the front of the studio. Next?" The woman had never looked at Katy's face.

Another earnest, trembly girl stepped forward into Katy's place. The registrar didn't look at her either.

Under the unnecessary (and slightly irritating) supervision of her mother, Katy filled out the form, which mostly asked for information already included on her resumé. Then she peeled off her sweatshirt and fidgeted as her mother took charge of attaching the "76" onto Katy's leotard.

"Are you sure you don't want me to stay?" Rebecca asked, her mouth full of safety pins.

"I'm sure."

"Because I can. There's an observation gallery right above the studio."

"I know, Mom. I'll be fine. Miss Emily is here. If I need anything, I can ask her." Katy's ballet teacher, Miss Emily, was famous for the volumes of minute, critical notes she took at auditions, and that was all the pressure Katy needed. She did not want her mother telling her afterwards that she didn't smile enough at the judges.

"All right, then." Rebecca said with poorly concealed relief. "If you're sure. I do have a lot of errands."

"I'm sure." The last pin was in place and Katy was securely labeled.

"Well, I have my cell phone with me if you need me. Otherwise I'll be back at 12:00."

"Okay. Bye." The lobby was emptying, and Katy was so anxious to get into the studio that she was almost hopping from one foot to the other.

"Do you have a snack with you?"

"Mo-omm! Yes! I gotta go in." Now she *was* hopping. Her mother kissed her lightly on the cheek.

"Bye, sweetie." They waved to each other, and Katy was on her own. She took a deep breath, shouldered her dance bag, and walked into the huge cavern of a studio.

She surveyed the room like a five-foot-tall general about to attack. A very nervous five-foot-tall general. With no army to back her up.

Like all ballet dancers, Katy had a keen sense for the subtle, implicit rules in a new environment. A mistake about where to leave your dance bag, what part of the barre belongs to the better dancers, whether skirts and leg warmers are forbidden or a fashion essential-- almost any false step can cost you credibility.

Protocol in an audition like this one, where applicants came from many different schools, is set by the dancers from the most prestigious schools; their strict dress codes and the arcane, ritualized etiquette of classical dance are drilled into them before they're old enough to read. Katy's school, The Ballet Conservatory, was considered one of the best in the city, so she wasn't worried about her hair or her clothes, but there was still the issue of where to stand at the barre.

She walked with careful casualness to the front of the studio and placed her form on the already hefty stack accumulating on the judges' table.

Her next move was to the side of the room where all the dance bags were shoved up against the wall out of the way. She sat down on the floor to put on her ballet slippers (hoping that no one would notice that her hands were still shaking) and evaluate the spaces still left open at the barres.

The unscheduled detour through the Jonathan Haskins Memorial Basement had eaten up a lot of minutes. It was now 8:50, and Katy hated arriving this late for an audition. She felt at a disadvantage right from the start. Most of the best dancers had arrived by 8:00 or 8:15, claimed the prime spots at the barres, and had had a leisurely period to stretch out and get comfortable in the room.

"Psst.. Katy!" came a loud whisper behind her. She turned and realized with a rush of relief that it was Jennifer Sandropol. She car-pooled with Jennifer to dance classes, and the girl got on Katy's very last nerve, but right at this moment, any familiar face was welcome, even Jennifer's.

"Hi, Jen. Who else is here?"

"Everybody. Brittany. Cynthia. Jessica. Meg. They're all over there together."

Jennifer pointed to the long barre attached to the wall directly across from the mirror. That was where Katy usually liked to stand, too. It allowed her to see herself sideways in the mirror for both sides of the exercises. "They'll let us squeeze in, if you want."

Katy thought about it for a moment. "Too crowded," she said finally. "And the studio is so big that if you stand there you're too far away from the mirror. And the judges' table."

"There's room at the side barres."

The very ends of the barres on the sides of the room were available, and some of the shyest dancers liked those because they felt less conspicuous. But let's face it, Katy thought, if you're going to be inconspicuous, why bother to come?

To Jennifer she said, "Miss Emily will kill us if we hide in the corner like that. We should take one of the portable barres in the center."

"Whatever," said Jennifer, standing up and adjusting the back of her leotard with a pop of the elastic. "But not right in front of the judges, okay? I never know where to look when they're right in my face like that."

Jennifer did a dorky imitation of a judge staring cross-eyed into Katy's face while taking notes. As usual she carried it way over the top, walking around Katy, looking her up and down, doing an unbelievably stupid monkey-walk. Several of the dancers stared around at them. One girl rolled her eyes. Katy was mortified.

"Stop it Jennifer!" she hissed. "And take your leg warmers off and spit out your gum. You look like you're trying out for cheerleader!" Katy stalked scornfully off with Jennifer trailing behind her, unfazed by Katy's disgust. At least in her irritation, Katy's hands had stopped shaking.

They found space together at a barre slightly off-center and started to stretch out. Katy did her best to look as though she didn't really know Jennifer, but she had a feeling that she had already been dropped in the mental trash can of everybody in the room.

At exactly 9:00 the accompanist took his place at the piano. At 9:10 the three adjudicators and the instructor entered. With their arrival, the hushed chatter and rustle of the dancers finally fell to tense silence.

This 9:00 am audition call was only for girls aged 11-13 with at least two years' training and a recommendation from an approved teacher (some more approved than others). There were 107 of them, filling every square foot of the studio.

Older girls would audition tomorrow morning, younger ones tomorrow afternoon, and later today the few interested boys would be looked at. Professional dancers were already under contract for the principal roles of Sugar Plum Fairy and her Cavalier, Snow Queen and her King, and Drosselmeyer. A few local celebrities and retired teachers, and even some of the dancers' parents (usually major contributors to the Dance Council) would be given non-dancing pantomime roles in the Party Scene.

This morning's audition, however, was the big one. From this audition the judges would cast Clara, the little girl whose mysterious Uncle Drosselmeyer gives her a nutcracker which comes to life and takes her on a magical adventure. Some of the best dancers from this group would also dance "Waltz of the Flowers" or Mirlitons, the toy flutes; some not quite as good would have minor parts in the Party Scene; many would not be cast at all.

But the plum, the prize, the dream of every girl in the room, was the part of Clara. Even though Clara had less actual dancing than some of the other roles, she was the star, the central figure around which the entire story of the ballet revolved, and tears would be shed when the part was cast. There would be one Clara, one hundred and six also-rans.

As 107 young dancers stood silently with tight smiles and nervous eyes, the judges introduced themselves and the instructor, a diminutive African-American ballerina named Tanya Quint, then seated themselves at the table at the front of the room. An assistant closed the studio door, and the audition began.

Ballet auditions are structured like ballet classes. They begin with the familiar

combinations at the barre: plié, tendu, dégagé.
But every teacher has characteristic ways of
combining movements into sequences, and it
takes a while to become accustomed to new ones.

Miss Quint began with fairly simple
combinations, gradually making them more
complicated and difficult as the girls relaxed a
little. Even so, Katy made a couple of errors in
the early combinations, using the wrong arm
position for a balance and forgetting a quick
weight-shift so she could change to her inside
foot.

Miss Quint was demonstrating the next
combination, and Katy was concentrating, so she
didn't actually see the man with the patch enter.
But she *felt* something. As though the air in the
room had turned to cold oil. As though something
nasty were crawling across her skin. It made her
stop and look behind herself.

ॐ

Across town, in the house on Wisteria Street,
Nijinska suddenly sat up.

Chapter 4:

Entrances and Exits

The man was spectacularly handsome in a lean, wolfish sort of way. Katy guessed him to be older than her father, probably much older, although it was hard to tell. His straight black hair had streaks of gray at the temples and he wore it long, pulled back into a thick ponytail at the nape of his neck. His olive skin looked even darker because of his immaculate white silk running suit. He wore a black patch over his right eye.

His looks were so dramatic that he needed a floor-length cape and a sword to balance them. He belonged on a huge black war-horse with medieval trappings of red and gold hanging from the saddle and bridle.

But as he moved into the room, Katy could feel the temperature drop and the air become unbreathable. Something about him was purely evil. Katy instinctively backed away from him as he crossed the studio.

༄

Across town, the fur on the back of Nijinska's neck stood straight up on end.

༄

Close beside the man with the patch, worn on his arm like a beautiful piece of jewelry, walked a ballerina. She was tall, reed-thin, with long mahogany-brown hair cascading down her back. Her skin was almost white, sun-sheltered all her life like a hot-house orchid; her neck was unnaturally long, and when she moved her head to look from side to side, it was with the shy hesitancy of a deer in the forest. Over black leggins she wore an oversized pale-peach pullover sweater that fell with careless grace off one porcelain shoulder. On her feet were black velvet flats that looked like ballet slippers but weren't. Katy thought that she was the most perfect creature she had ever seen--except for her dark green eyes. Her eyes were vacant and empty, like a room with the lights turned off.

The judges and the man with the patch greeted each other warmly. Miss Quint nodded and smiled. The ballerina did not speak or make any sign of recognition. One of the judges stood and introduced the two newcomers to the dancers as Hugh Langford, Artistic Director for *The Nutcracker* and Lise Moreau, who would dance the Snow Queen in the long waltz at the end of Act I.

Mr. Langford held Lise's chair as she seated herself at the table's end. He sat between her and the judges, one hand resting lightly on her shoulder. The odd blankness in Lise Moreau's dark eyes twisted into something like pain as Hugh Langford's fingers touched the bit of white shoulder not covered by her sweater.

The disturbing sense of evil that Katy had felt when Mr. Langford entered the room dissolved as quickly as it had arrived, and she was sure now that she had imagined it. Probably just a reaction to the stress of the audition. Katy shook her head slightly to clear it and told herself to get a grip.

Fortunately Miss Quint decided to start again teaching the next combination, and Katy was able to concentrate on that.

As the barre continued, Miss Quint gave the better dancers a few corrections, her coffee-colored eyes winked and twinkled, and she teased them with little jokes about their mistakes.

Katy herself received two corrections--a simple clarification of a leg position that she had misunderstood, and a much more sophisticated one about her turnout (her least favorite subject). The weakest dancers were given no corrections at all. One of the harsher realities of pre-professional dance training is that teachers can't waste a lot of time trying to improve a hopeless dancer. In fact, Katy had once glimpsed a small poster inside a teacher's locker at her studio that read:

"Never try to teach a pig to sing.

It wastes your time and annoys the pig."

It was a cold-blooded way of phrasing a hard truth: that a teacher's class time and personal energy were limited and must be invested where it will produce the best results. Katy was just grateful not to be considered one of the pigs.

By the time the last of the barre exercises was over and the girls were told to "Do your own stretch," Katy felt that her audition was going well. She had almost managed to screen out of her mind the judges as they peered carefully at the dancers' numbers and wrote occasional comments on applications, now and again asking a whispered question of Hugh Langford to which he would respond with a nod or an impatient shake of the head.

Perhaps hardest of all, she had also managed to ignore the stupid faces Jennifer made every time Miss Quint gave a tricky exercise. Katy swore to herself that she would stand as far away as possible from Jennifer during center.

Center, the part of the audition where they would come away from the barres, was also where she could begin to get a feel for how well she was doing relative to the other dancers, or as Miss Emily put it, "where you stand in the food chain."

Center combinations were taught to the whole group and then danced in smaller groups, so Katy would be able to watch the other dancers better than she could at the barre. Still, even in small groups, she couldn't imagine how the judges could look carefully at each of these 107 dancers and still have them out of there by noon.

"Please move the barres to the sides of the room," said Miss Quint, "then give me your attention for a moment."

As one of the judges rose, a stack of papers in his hand, Jennifer gasped, "Are they making cuts?"

Katy felt a cold fist in her stomach, and all her confidence about her dancing vanished in a heartbeat. Cuts? Already? It was true. The judges usually eliminated some girls before the end, but she hadn't thought it would be so early-- before they even danced a single step in the center!

Katy's mind ran a high-speed instant replay of all the tiny mistakes she had made at the barre. Every moment when she had let her face go blank or even frowned, all those little concentration slips when she hadn't paid close enough attention to the combination, every time when she had not pushed her leg quite as high as she could have or had relaxed her balance before the very last note of the music died out--they all came back to haunt her like guilty ghosts.

The judge cleared his throat. "If I call your number, you may go. The rest of you please continue to stretch while we place you in groups for center. The following numbers are through for the day: numbers 5, 6, 12, 15..."

The judges' list seemed to drone on forever, eliminating about thirty dancers in the same bored tone of voice he would have used to read any list of meaningless numbers. The difference lay in the fact that these numbers were pinned over the loudly beating hearts of the young girls who were being told--publicly--that they were not good enough and not wanted.

Katy listened carefully through the entire list, not trusting the numerical order. What if they called her number out of order and she missed it and stayed when she wasn't supposed to? They might call her by name or walk over to her and tell her to leave, and she would have to walk out all alone, and she was sure she would cry. In fact, she was sure she would cry anyway.

Katy concentrated so hard on hearing the numbers that she didn't move or even breathe until the list was all read. They had not called number 76. She was sure of that. She exhaled.

She slid easily down into a split and began stretching, watching out of the corner of her eye as the girls whose numbers had been called walked hastily to gather up their dance bags and slink out the door. Their painful embarrassment made an echoing ache in Katy's own heart. Most had their heads down, trying not to cry.

"How awful not to even make the first cut!" Katy whispered to Jennifer.

"What if their mothers aren't coming back until noon?" Jennifer whispered back. "What if they have to just sit there in the lobby for two hours?"

The two girls cringed at the thought, and Katy said a silent prayer of thanks that her mother had a cell phone.

"Did anybody from our class get cut?" Katy said. Miss Emily was too savvy to send an unqualified student to an audition, and every girl from their class who had been given permission to audition had a legitimate shot at a part. But you never knew.

"Of course not," said Jennifer, smug and supercilious now that she had survived the cut. "They didn't cut any *real* dancers."

And now that she looked carefully, Katy could see that most of the girls who were leaving didn't have that ballet "look." They were a little heavy or dressed differently. A few had short hair.

The remaining girls were all little cookie-cutter ballerinas. The world of professional ballet is an extremely conservative one that quickly encourages rebels and rugged individualists to investigate jazz or modern dance.

"Check out the girl with the green back pack," Jennifer said. "She's wearing *black* ballet slippers! She's not getting cut--she's getting hauled off by the fashion police."

"Jennifer, that is so cold!" Katy said; but she giggled a little as she said it. Part of Katy did feel for the girls in the sad parade of failure heading out the studio door. But she was honest enough to admit feeling a small glow of superiority, too.

She looked around at the other lean, elongated bodies stretching out across the floor with their identically perfect not-a-wisp-out-of-place buns and their identical black leotard/pink tights uniforms. Katy saw the same emotional mixture reflected in their eyes: one part pity and one part "well what did they *expect?*"

Suddenly one of the exiting girls turned around in the doorway and reversed direction, shouldering her way through the pack of rejected dancers like a salmon heading upstream. She looked almost too young to be there--or maybe she was just very short for her age. She might have been Native American or perhaps Hispanic, with dark almond eyes and straight black hair worn in pigtails instead of a bun, making her look even younger. She had the rounded muscles of a little soccer player, not the long thin muscles considered ideal for ballet dancers, and she bounced a little as she walked.

The room went dead silent as she marched back across the enormous studio to the judges' table. There was a twinkle of tears in her eyes, but she gravely shook the hands of each of the judges, Mr. Langford, and Miss Quint, thanking them for the audition.

Then she walked, chin high, pigtails bobbing, the huge length of the studio and disappeared out the door.

"Wow," whispered Katy. "Who was that?"

"Samantha Mia," whispered Jennifer. "She takes at Miss Jimmie's." Katy recognized the name of the school. It was popular with girls who liked jazz and wanted to go out for drill team, but it did a poor job of training ballet students.

"Watch out for that one," Katy overheard another girl say. "She'll be back."

Chapter 5:

Illusions

The center-floor part of the audition began. There was an extra-slow adagio that was simple to learn but difficult to execute smoothly. Then two different petit allégro combinations. Katy didn't like the small jumps because she wasn't particularly strong or quick in the air; her long legs always seemed to drag just slightly behind the music.

Her emotional state yoyo-ed up and down as she watched the other dancers and tried to figure out where she ranked in the group. After adagio she calculated that she was probably in the top ten or fifteen dancers. After petit allégro she felt like she'd be lucky if they even let her buy a ticket to the show.

The pirouette combination suited her better, after which the judges made another cut. This one was somehow less emotionally wrenching than the first, even though two of Katy's friends were eliminated. Now about fifty girls were left in the studio.

Miss   Quint   gave   three   more   center combinations: a diagonal of turns from the corner, a grand allégro with big jumps and a double pirouette, and a long révérance with wonderfully romantic port de bras linking a series of graceful curtseys. Then the dancers were given a five-minute break to get a drink of water, go to the bathroom, or grab a snack.

Half a dozen of Katy's classmates clustered around the water fountain, releasing their pent-up tension in rapid-fire whispers.

"So what do you think?"

"I think I should have faked a sprained ankle before that grand allégro. Did you see me hop the landing on the pirouette?"

"Did you check out the extension on that girl from Metropolitan? What's her name?"

"Michelle Something. But she can't turn."

"With legs like that she doesn't need to."

"So how about Hugh Langford?   Gorgeous or *what*?"

The conversation dissolved into appreciative whistles and sighs and fake faints. Clearly no one but Katy had felt that about-to-crawl-out-of-your-skin feeling, and Katy told herself firmly that she had just had a bad case of audition paranoia.

The last hour was reserved for learning actual choreography from *The Nutcracker*, taught by Mr. Langford himself. As he began demonstrating a lovely (but difficult) section from "Waltz of the Flowers," many of the girls exchanged glances and mischievous grins. There was even a some subtle maneuvering for the positions closest to the front of the room (and therefore closest to the director).

Langford now seemed nothing at all like
Katy's first impression of him. He was warm and
funny and charming, with a gift for somehow
getting each dancer to jump higher and balance
longer than she ever had before. There was an
infectious energy and excitement about him that
lit them up from inside. One girl did a triple
pirouette for the first time in her life, and he
laughed heartily and applauded her.

They worked on the waltz for forty minutes.
After that there was only one last thing in the
audition: a   pantomime   scene   in   which
Drosselmeyer   gives   Clara   the   enchanted
nutcracker as her Christmas present.

The fifty girls were shown the scene, and in
groups of ten acted out the scene with imaginary
partners. Five groups, ten Claras in each group
with   ten   invisible   Drosselmeyers   and   ten
imaginary nutcrackers.

Katy was in the last group, and when they
finished, Hugh Langford was not entirely pleased.
He   paced   among   them,   his   voice   saddened,
reluctantly admitting his disappointment.

"The steps are all very correct," he conceded,
"but you're not *performing* it. Where is the magic?
The sense of mystery? I want you to make me
understand that this gift is not just any present,
not just a pair of socks from your grandmother!"
They all laughed. "But that it is an extraordinary
gift, a once-in-a-lifetime gift. More than a gift--an
enchantment! Because of this extraordinary gift,
Clara's life will never, never be the same. Here,
like this."

He reached out and took Katy's hand, leading
her to the center of the room. "What is your
name, my dear?" he asked, smiling at her. Her
heart almost stopped.

"Katy Moon."

He continued his explanation to the room. "When Drosselmeyer gives you the nutcracker, I want to feel as though it is making your hands tingle. As though you feel it growing warm and alive in your hand. How would that make you feel, Miss Moon?"

"Frightened," she giggled.

"Exactly!" he said. "Excited *and* a little frightened. Now show me. Here is my gift to you." He closed his hands around Katy's hands. Their eyes met, and she knew that she would dance until her feet bled if it would please this man. The accompanist began the music, and Katy started to play the scene.

As Katy/Clara received the imaginary nutcracker from Langford/Drosselmeyer, her eyes glowed with the thrill of the enchanted gift. She drew back from it a bit as though a little afraid of it. She lifted it above her head and waltzed delightedly around in a circle with it, laughing. She rushed back to him to thank him with a loving hug.

To Katy's delighted astonishment, Langford picked her up and lifted her high in the air, and she was soaring off into space, feather-light, in perfect control, released for once from the tyranny of physics...

Hugh Langford's head suddenly snapped upward and to the right.

There, in the window of the observation gallery, amid the cluster of mothers and teachers, stood a tiny figure in brightly-colored silk patches. Mrs. Pye stared down at the man with the patch as he held Katy high above him like a prize he had claimed.

Langford held Katy in mid-air as he locked eyes with the old woman. The silk patches billowed as though a wind were blowing through them. Layers of her skirts floated up behind her like wide wings. Mrs. Pye seemed to contain a light within her, a rose-colored radiance, so that the gallery and the mothers and teachers disappeared in the dark behind her.

Katy slowly, fearfully, turned her head back to look at Hugh Langford.

And she *saw.*

Something crawled under his skin. Something rotten. Something decayed with unimaginable age. Something evil.

Katy wanted to scream, but all she could do was choke. She wanted to fight herself loose, but she was frozen in fear.

Langford's eyes narrowed and blazed in anger as he stared up at Mrs. Pye. Katy heard a low, canine growl come from his throat. He slowly lowered Katy to the floor where she stumbled back from him.

The illusion was instantly gone. Hugh Langford was a handsome dark-haired choreographer. Mrs. Pye was a tiny old lady in a gaudy dress.

Langford smiled at Katy and then said apologetically to the room, "I should know better than to lift a dancer without warning her first. Sorry, Miss Moon. Entirely my fault." And he winked at her.

"That's okay," Katy stammered. Almost worse than her blinding fear was an overwhelming sense of loss, of grief. As though she had touched for a moment some miraculous thing that she longed for--needed--beyond all else, and it had crumbled away in her hand. She felt like she might faint, and Mr. Langford took hold of her arm to steady her.

"But the thing to remember," said Hugh Langford, speaking to the room, but looking straight at Katy as he still held her arm with one inescapable hand, "is that magic is a powerful and dangerous thing. Clara senses this when she accepts the gift. But she does accept it. She *commits* herself to it.   And that... changes everything."

He released her and walked away.

Katy remembered nothing more about the audition. Surely they repeated the scene. There was probably a short speech from the judges thanking them and telling them when the casting lists would be posted. Katy didn't remember.

The next thing she knew she was standing in the lobby with her mother saying yes, the audition went fine... no, she wasn't hungry... yes, she was fine. Just very tired and she wanted to go home and lie down, please.

As the car pulled out of the parking lot, dark thunderheads were gathering over the city, building toward an unexpected electrical storm.

ℰ

When Katy got home, Nijinska was pacing back and forth in her bedroom. There was a rip in the bedroom curtain, and the glass in the window was scratched as though the cat had tried urgently to get out the window.

Katy and Nijinska curled up together into one small ball of girl and cat, and held each other until they both stopped shaking and fell asleep under the thunder rolling high across the city.

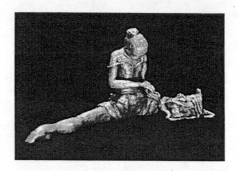

Chapter 6:

The Most Extraordinary Child

For Katy Moon, disturbing and inexplicable visions were, if not commonplace, at least familiar. And in the past, when she had tried to talk about what she had seen, the results had not been good.

There had been, for example, the incident at the zoo when she was six and a half. On a sunny August afternoon Katy had stopped, transfixed and trembling, in front of an elephant whom she knew was grieving, fatally depressed over the loss of his mate. Katy had tried through her sobs to explain to her mother that the animal was going to die and please, *please!* couldn't they *do* something? Katy became hysterical, Rebecca became first impatient and then furious, and they had never been back to the zoo.

There was the period even earlier when Katy noticed that there was an extra color that nobody talked about--something past purple which seemed to occur only in plants and animals, never on things that were man-made. When she would point to it and ask what color it was, everyone said that it was gray. But it wasn't. Rebecca took Katy to the ophthalmologist after that discussion.

And more and more frequently, in the last year particularly, there had been instances similar in nature to her Saturday experience in which Katy had glimpsed people who *were* quite different from what they *seemed*.

The most vivid had been a homeless man standing on a street corner downtown holding his cap out for people to give him spare change. Rebecca had pulled Katy across the street to avoid him, but something about him drew Katy's eye. As she and her mother waited at the traffic light, Katy thought she saw a gold light around him, and as she looked harder, under his battered, defeated outer face she saw what she described to herself as his "true" face. It was beautiful and strong, and Katy understood that he had come there not to beg for handouts but to teach passers-by something about themselves by how they reacted to him. She hadn't even attempted to explain that one to her mother.

Gradually Katy had learned to cautiously assess what she saw, to decide whether or not anyone else probably saw it, and if no one else did, to keep it to herself. It never occurred to her to worry that she was crazy; some inner compass told her that she wasn't. But these things she saw made the people she loved angry or ill-at-ease, put in jeopardy their affection and approval. She just preferred not to mention them.

So after the audition, she said nothing to anyone. By Saturday night her mood had lifted in spite of the violent thunderstorm that had knocked out their electricity and rattled their windows all night. By Monday morning she had filed the memory away in the same mental box

with her extra color and had gone on with her
ordinary, everyday life.

Tuesday morning, when she came across the
yellowed piece of crumbling paper in the bottom of
her dance bag, she had to think a long moment
before she remembered where it had come from.
It looked very old. The spidery script with its odd
spellings was difficult to decipher, but it intrigued
her. She sat on her bed and started to puzzle out
the words.

ॐ

15 August
Padua, Italy
I have seen the most extraordinary child today.

*Just after luncheon I called at the studios of a
sculptor recommended to me by my cousin Arianne.
Having no patron at present, the man works and
lives rather squalidly above a foul-smelling butcher
shop in the market district. How he tolerates the
stench and the noise, I cannot fathom. These
artists have remarkable stomachs.*

*Holding a well-perfumed handkerchief to guard
my poor nose, and in mortal fear for my bones as I
climbed his rickety stairs, I found the poor beggar,
all over mud from boots to bonnet, hard at work on
a clay maquette of a dancing child.*

*In the center of the room, barefoot upon a rough
wooden platform which raised her three feet in the
air, was his child model, a black-eyed urchin of
perhaps eleven years of age. The pose required
her to stand arched backwards at the waist, her
chin tipped skyward, the tangled masses of her
black curls falling below her waist, holding her
skirts out with both hands, the left hand slightly in
front of her, the right slightly behind. A lovely pose,
quite animated and graceful. I hope the poor
wretch of a sculptor can capture it.*

I signaled to him to continue working and pulled a rough wooden chair over to a window where I could catch the afternoon breeze and observe the work with the light behind me.

Even now, at this remove, the look of the child haunts me. In the summer heat, her bare arms and legs glistened with sweat, and she trembled with the effort of holding the difficult position for long periods, but she never moved without permission.

When he allowed her to, she would silently accept a cup of water from his hand, crouch down beneath a low table like an animal in its lair, stretch out her cramped muscles, and stare out at me with fearful black eyes until told to resume her position.

The odd conceit gradually formed itself in my head that the dirty little thing was a form of breathing, moving sculpture! I fear the heat and the butcher's noxious fumes have addled me

࿇

"Katy!"   Her mother's voice finally broke through her concentration.

"Yes, ma'am?"

"Answer me when I call you! You're going to be late!"

"Sorry! Coming!"

When she returned home from her ballet class that night, the yellowed page was no longer on her bed.   But Katy was tired, and she fell asleep without noticing.

Chapter 7:

And the Winner Is...

Wednesday after school she rode to the studio as usual with Jennifer Sandropol. Also as usual, they had an argument on the way there.

"Jennifer, that is *so* not true," Katy declared flatly.

"It is. I heard Ms. Shanahan say it." Sandra Shanahan was the owner and director of Ballet Conservatory where Katy had taken dance since the age of three.

"You heard Ms. Shanahan say that Miss Emily was doing Arabian."

"That's right."

"Miss Emily."

"Yeah."

"Our teacher, Miss Emily."

"Yes, Katy!"

"The Arabian variation."

"Yeah!"

"In *The Nutcracker*."

"Yesss! I was walking past the office door, and Ms. Shanahan was on the phone, and she said that Miss Emily was doing Arabian!"

Jennifer lived to gossip, but she hardly ever got her facts right.

"You heard this. Through the office door."

"Yesssss!"

"You did not." Katy's dismissal was complete and disdainful.

"Want to bet?" Jennifer challenged.

"How much?"

"Five dollars."

Katy considered carefully. She certainly did not want to have to pay Jennifer Sandropol five dollars under any circumstances, but this was a sure thing. Miss Emily was one of the best teachers around, but she had to be at least fifty years old--far past the age when she could be considered for a dancing role. "It's a bet," she said.

"Five dollars?"

"Yes, Jennifer. Five dollars."

"Okay. My mom's a witness." Jennifer's tone managed to imply that Katy might try to weasel out of the deal. Jennifer was such a pain.

The two girls stared out opposite car windows, each miffed at the other, until the car pulled up in front of the studio. They piled out, heaving dance bags onto shoulders, and walked in the front door, where they were both stopped dead in their tracks.

The lobby of the Conservatory was usually busy, but in a politely hushed sort of way. Today it had taken on all the attributes of a train wreck.

A crowd of students of all ages was packed six deep around the bulletin board. Several girls were jumping up and down, squealing and hugging each other. Off in a corner, one girl was crying silently. And at the reception desk an irate mother was demanding to see Ms. Shanahan and saying loudly to Betty, the much-abused school secretary, "...she will *not* be a mouse! She was a mouse last year and we couldn't even see her face under that stupid mask!"

Katy and Jennifer took in the bedlam in one glance and said in unison, "It's posted!"

Fifteen minutes later, Katy was sitting alone on the dressing room floor trying to sort out her feelings. When she had wormed her way close enough to the board to read the cast list, the first thing she had read was the line that said: "Clara - Brianna Wells."

Katy knew the girl by sight, although they went to different dance schools. Brianna was an average dancer with enormous blue eyes and white-blond hair that fell in ringlets when she took down her bun. She was beautiful, but far from being the best dancer at the audition, and Katy had even been a little surprised that she had survived the last round of cuts.

The next thing Katy had looked at was the list of dancers in "Waltz of the Flowers." Katy's name was not listed there or in the Party Scene as Friends of Clara either, and for a few horrified moments she thought she had not been cast at all. In a near-panic she scanned the long list until, almost by accident, she saw her name listed at the bottom of "Waltz of the Snowflakes."

Now she sat in the dressing room, as far as possible from the other girls who were congratulating each other or saying things (some sincere and some phony as a three-dollar bill) like, "I can't see why they cast Gina and not you. You were *so* much better."

Jennifer bounced over to her, an unwelcome intrusion on her misery.

"I got 'Waltz of the Flowers!' What did you get?"

" 'Snow.' "

"You did not!"

Katy sighed with exasperation. She was in no mood for this. "I did, too, Jennifer. Go read the board."

"It's on pointe."

"Remember last year? There were four girls from the class ahead of ours who were sort of Attendants for the Snow Queen?"

Jennifer's eyes narrowed as she struggled to understand what Katy was talking about. Jennifer was an awfully dim bulb sometimes. "Oh yeaahhh... So is that good? Better than 'Flowers?' "

Katy shrugged. "Last year the Attendants mostly just stood in B+ and did port de bras while the girls on pointe danced."

"Maybe they thought you had nice arms." If Jennifer was trying to be encouraging, Katy thought the attempt a little lame.

"Yeah," Katy said sarcastically. "Or maybe they were afraid I'd trip and kill some *real* dancer if they gave me actual dancing to do." Katy was a bit embarrassed at sounding so jealous, but she didn't know how to retract it once it was out of her mouth.

She stood up and headed for the door. Jennifer didn't follow her, which was fine with Katy. She just wanted barre to start so she could forget about the cast list.

After ten years of ballet classes, Katy was deeply addicted to barre. It was her refuge, her Zen-like retreat from the world. During barre, absolutely nothing existed for her except the feel of her muscles, her reflection in the mirror, the music, and Miss Emily's voice. She always welcomed that retreat, and some days she even needed it. Today was one of those days.

Katy had to wait a few moments in the
hallway for the earlier class of younger students
to finish their révérance. The crowd around the
bulletin board had thinned a little, but the angry
mother was still arguing with poor Betty, saying,
"...and I do *not* pay you over $100 a month to have
her hop around the stage with a *sack* over her
head! Her grandmother flew across the country to
see her last year and we couldn't even tell which
mouse she was!"

Betty seemed to be shriveling, hunching her
shoulders and getting lower and lower behind the
desk. Miss Shanahan, the school director, made
it a point every year to be "in a meeting" for the 48
hours after the *Nutcracker* cast was posted,
leaving poor Betty to absorb the brunt of the
abuse from unhappy mothers. In Katy's opinion,
whatever Betty was getting paid, it wasn't enough.

When the class of ten-year-olds were
dismissed, Katy was the first one in the door. She
stood in her usual spot, put her leg on the barre
and leaned forward over it, hiding her face on her
thigh. Eventually the other girls trickled in, still
chatting about *Nutcracker*. As their teacher
entered and walked to the front of the room, the
volume dropped to a whisper, but didn't stop
entirely.

"All right, ladies," Miss Emily said calmly,
"you may resume charting your career paths after
class." Everyone laughed and then fell quickly
silent.

"Pliés," continued Miss Emily, using her
familiar, rapid-fire classroom shorthand of French
terms and hand movements to describe the
movement combinations, "preparation one, two.
Two demi's, two grand, port de bras forward and
up, relevé, lower the heels. Same thing in second

with port de bras into the barre, fourth, away, fifth back. Balance in sou-sus, turn second side."

The music began, and Katy gave herself over to the demands of the exercise. Miss Emily had been her ballet teacher for three years now, and as far as Katy was concerned, she was the perfect combination of rigorous disciplinarian and affectionate friend. She took her students very seriously, pushing them to the absolute limit of their abilities, but when those limits were reached, she laughed with them at their failures, telling them that "just because you couldn't do it that time doesn't mean you can't do it the next time, so try it again."

Students left Miss Emily's class exhausted, but they hardly ever left in tears. Katy adored her.

The class proceeded as always, with Miss Emily prowling up and down the lines of dancers, sometimes calling the steps out or counting the music aloud, sometimes reminding them of technical points, often adjusting a student's position as she passed, lifting or lowering an arm, pressing the tip of a finger into a muscle to remind them to straighten or tighten or elongate something.

After forty-five minutes, barre gave way to center, and after center it was time for the thirty-minute pointe class.

"You have three minutes to change shoes, ladies," said Miss Emily. "Do it quickly." There was a controlled dash to their dance bags.

Katy dug out her lamb's wool, took a small scrap from the box, and stretched it around her toes. In the Conservatory, the bulkier but more comfortable "bunny pads" were forbidden, and some teachers sneered at any padding at all in the pointe shoes, but Miss Emily allowed a tiny ration of lamb's wool.

The idea was to use as little as possible, providing a bit of protection against blisters while still allowing your feet to "feel the floor." It was the unanimous opinion of the students that there was absolutely no possibility of ever feeling anything through the layers of satin and glue that formed the box of the pointe shoe. It was like wearing pink satin bricks on your feet. But Katy took it on faith that if she did it correctly, sooner or later, she would in fact feel the floor.

So much of ballet was like that. For two years your teacher told you, "A pirouette is just a balance that goes around. Go to passé, close your arms, spot, and let yourself go around." For two years you do all those things and either haul yourself around with a sort of twisty jerking motion or fall right on your butt. Then suddenly, one day, whizzz! A perfect floating single pirouette. And you realize with blinding clarity that, indeed, "a pirouette is just a balance that goes around!"

After years of these "Ah hah!" experiences, Katy had learned to follow instructions and trust. Maybe today she would feel the floor. Or maybe tomorrow.

"Hey, Moon!" came a whisper from a girl named Cindy sitting behind her. "Congratulations!"

Katy looked back. "Thanks," she said, and even managed a smile. She found she was now able to be a little gracious if someone congratulated her on being cast. Even if she *was* just an Attendant in 'Snow.'

"What'd she get?" she heard another girl ask.

"Understudy for Clara," whispered Cindy.

"Cool," said the second girl, "Way to go, Katy."

Katy wasn't able to respond this time. Her brain had locked. Her whole body had gone numb. Understudy for Clara? Was that possible? How could she conceivably have missed reading that?

She glanced quickly at Miss Emily, opening her mouth to ask for permission to go to the restroom so she could check the bulletin board on the way. But the bulletin board was visible from the classroom, and Miss Emily could wither you with one raised eyebrow if she suspected you of skipping part of class. Katy decided not to risk it.

Her concentration failed her this time. She went mechanically through échappés, her mind on the cast list tacked to the board just a tantalizing few feet from where she stood. Fifth position, slide to second. Fifth position, slide to second. She had no idea whether or not she felt the floor.

Thirty minutes dragged by. The last pointe exercise came and went, a long diagonal of bourrées led by Miss Emily, whose feet made a silent pink blur as they sped across the floor. The students clumped grimly after her, their pink bricks working as fast as they possibly could, which is to say: not very.

The last curtsey was followed by the traditional applause for the teacher. Katy held the last position for the minimum acceptable five seconds before she bolted for the door. Crossing the short distance to the bulletin board, she almost bowled over a four-year old escapee from the baby class who was making an emergency dash to the bathroom.

At the bottom of the last page was the section she had overlooked. Under the heading "Understudies" was listed, sure enough, "Understudy for Clara: Katy Moon."

Katy stood and stared at the typewritten line for a long, long time. It was true. She had been cast as an understudy for the part she wanted with her whole heart. She was the back-up for a girl whose main qualification as a dancer seemed to be her long blond ringlets. *And* she had a second part in piece with a group of dancers older and more advanced than she was. But in a role that probably didn't require her to do more than stand and wave her arms around. Now she *really* didn't know how to feel.

Jennifer Sandropol came up behind her and handed her a fat brown envelope. "Here. I got your rehearsal packet. Your mom's car is out front. You ready to go?"

"In a second." Katy quickly scanned the lists, looking for the name she needed. "Ahem," she coughed significantly, pointing to "Arabian." "Miss Emily is not either doing Arabian. You owe me $5."

"It just so happens," said Jennifer in her most obnoxiously arrogant tone, "that I *asked* Miss Emily, and she's *setting* Arabian. So you owe *me* $5."

"I do not, Jennifer Sandropol! You bet she was dancing it!"

"Nuh uh! I bet she was *doing* it. Setting it is doing it!"

"It is *so* not!"

By working hard at it, they were able to make the argument last them all the way to Jennifer's house, so Katy did not tell her mother about the casting until dinner.

Her mother said nice Mom-things, but Katy could tell from the flat look in her eyes that she wasn't particularly impressed. Rebecca took the thick packet of information and buried herself in the logistical details of rehearsals and performances, leaving Katy to poke at her meatloaf and peas and mashed potatoes in silence.

She wished that her father were home for dinner for a change instead of working late. Even the twins would have been a welcome diversion, but they were sharing a bad cold and were tucked up in their room sleeping it off.

"It says here you do get to perform Clara for a Saturday matinee," said Rebecca without looking up from the papers. "We'll get tickets for that one."

Katy was too depressed to say anything more than a very small, "Okay."

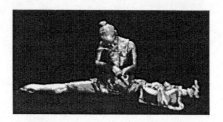

Chapter 8:

Two Moons at Midnight

By the time Michael Moon's car pulled into the driveway on Wisteria Street late that night, all the female occupants of the house were tucked away in their separate bedrooms. Katy, however, was lying awake, thinking about things, and she heard the garage door open.

She padded softly down the stairs, barefoot and wearing her big sleep T-shirt, and met her father in the kitchen. Nijinska followed closely behind her.

"Hi, Daddy," she called quietly.

"Hi, Elfin Princess of the Night," Michael smiled. "What are you doing up?"

"I couldn't sleep. And now I'm hungry." Nijinska meowed once. "So is Nij."

"Well, let's see," he said, opening the fridge, "we have leftovers (something that looks like meatloaf) and... and... other leftovers (something that looks like not-meatloaf). Which do you want?"

Katy ducked under his arm that was holding the fridge door, leaned against him, and peered into the sparkling glass and chrome interior. "Peanut butter sandwich."

"Me too. Jelly?"

"Yes, please."

"Milk?"

"Uh huh."

"And... and....???"

They looked at each other conspiratorially and said together, "Potato chips!" Potato chips crunched up into peanut butter and jelly was a secret addiction for them both, forbidden by Rebecca Moon who found it too disgusting to tolerate.

They sat down together at the kitchen table with their illegal snacks (plus a slice of cheese for Nijinska) and proceeded to eat the evidence.

For once Michael Moon did not have a stack of papers in front of him or a telephone glued to his ear, and Katy was able to actually tell him the news about her *Nutcracker* roles. He seemed to be more interested (but less knowledgeable) about it than her mother, and Katy shyly explained that she didn't really know if she had done well or poorly.

"Well, let's analyze this," said Michael, his mouth full of sweet-and-salt sandwich. "Did a lot of people try out?"

"*Audition*, Daddy. You try out for cheerleader. You audition for a ballet. And yes, lots of kids."

"Just your school or lots of schools?"

"Lots of schools. From all over the city and some from other towns even."

"And does everybody who tries out--pardon me, auditions--get in?"

"No.   About eight kids from my class auditioned. Two got Party Scene, which isn't very good. Three got 'Waltz of the Flowers.' And there was me. Two didn't get anything."

"And from the other schools?"

"There are maybe two other schools where most of the kids made it. Out of the girls from the rest of the schools, mostly just little kids got in. And I think every boy who auditioned got something."

Her father nodded solemnly. "Supply and demand. Ok, let me ask you this: is it your school that puts this show on? Do they have any reason to choose students from your school over some other school? Other than the quality of the dancers, I mean."

"No. It's put on by the Dance Council. They hire people who don't work for any of the schools to direct it. The judges are from out of town."

He thought for a long moment. "Well, here's what it sounds like to me. Out of the dance students available in this city, they judged you to be," he held up two fingers and ticked off his points, "first, good enough to be cast at all. Second, good enough to get a dancing role instead of just an extra in the parade..."

"The Party Scene, Daddy."

"Whatever. So that puts you in maybe the top 10% of dance students your age in the city. Which is good. Actually very good. But your question is now, 'How good am I relative to the ones who are plants?' "

"Flowers, Daddy. *Flowers*. But yeah, I guess so."

"My answer is: you probably don't have enough data to answer that."

"Oh, Daddy!"

"I know that's not the answer you want, but it's true. You got a part that's a little ambiguous."

"What does that mean?"

"That it can be interpreted more than one way. And it sounds like the part of Clarissa..."

"Clara!" She laughed and punched his arm.

"Whatever. This is a very important role, but it's not cast necessarily just for your dancing ability. Like maybe your stage presence, or the way you look, or your acting ability is more important. Right?"

"I guess so. But then there's the 'Snow' thing."

"Well, that could be because of the fact that you're understudying Claudia."

"Clara."

"And maybe that's what works out best with the practice schedule."

"Rehearsal schedule. Yeah, maybe. But I wish I knew."

"Yep, I'm sure you do. Uncertainty is an uncomfortable thing. Life is full of it. Welcome to the real world. But I think it's also true that you shouldn't minimize the importance of whatever quality they saw in you that made them cast you as Clara. Speaking not as an artist, but as a consumer of art, I would much prefer to watch a performer who has great presence on-stage than one who can do lots of technical tricks."

The two of them were to the point of picking up the last potato chip crumbs with their fingertips, licking the salt off each finger as they did. It had been the best (and longest) conversation Katy had had with her father in years--certainly since he had gotten his last promotion at work. She began to wonder if it might be possible to broach the topic that concerned her even more than the *Nutcracker* issues: Mrs. Pye and Hugh Langford. She had an idea how to start, but wasn't sure she could finish. She decided against it.

With one slightly sticky finger she reached over and touched the corner of her father's eyebrow where it flicked up into a "wing" like her own.

"We have the same eyebrows, don't we, Daddy?"

"We absolutely do. I got mine from my grandmother, Maggie Moon. You got yours from me."

"My great-grandmother had them, too?"

"Yes she did. I have a couple of old photographs I'll show you sometime."

"What was she like?"

"Gramma Moon was... different. Very different." Michael Moon chuckled at a private memory.

"Different how?"

"Well, no one wanted to talk about it much," Michael confided, "in fact, one of the worst spankings I ever got in my life was for telling one of my mother's friends that my grandmother had 'powers.' But that's what Gramma Moon claimed herself. Used to drive my mother up the wall."

Katy suddenly got very serious. "What kind of powers?"

"You have to understand, Katy, that my grandparents were very simple, country people. Good people. Hard-working, kind. But uneducated and superstitious. And ignorant people are sometimes inclined to interpret things they don't understand as being supernatural. But I was Gramma Moon's favorite grandchild; she used to say she and I were 'two peas in a pod.' And she used to tell me these wild stories about how she was a 'seer,' whatever that meant, and that I was one, too.

"There was even a period, when I was about 13 or maybe 14, that I started to think I was having 'visions' like Gramma Moon. I let it slip to my mother one day, and she put a stop to that."

"What did she do?"

"She kept me from going to see Gramma Moon for a while. Then made sure that she was always with me when we visited." Michael looked a little sad at the memory. "It was pretty hard on me. I loved that old lady, and at that age sometimes I felt like Gramma was the only person in my world who really *knew* me.... But by the time I was old enough to make my own decisions about it, she had died."

"But the powers..." Katy started again.

At which moment, her father's cell phone rang. He answered it, "Moon," listened a moment and, covering the mouthpiece with his hand, said, "Sorry, Elf. I have to take this overseas call. You better scoot up to bed."

Katy stalled for a long while, putting their plates and glasses into the dishwasher, putting away the peanut butter jar and the chips, cleaning crumbs from the table and the countertop. When she had done everything there was to do in the kitchen (and even faked some extra stuff) her father was still deeply involved in some discussion about "the Brussels project."

She waited, leaning against the kitchen counter, Nijinska rubbing against her ankles, until Michael Moon picked up his briefcase, pulled out a thick manila folder, and said into the phone, "Okay, well, I have those documents right here. Let's go through them together point by point and make sure we understand what the problem is, okay?"

Katy kissed him on top of the little bald spot on the back of his head. He squeezed her arm and winked good-night. She picked up her cat and headed for her room.

Climbing into bed, she saw Nijinska, with an uncharactistic spurt of energy, make a quick dash toward the bed, arch her back, and, with a hiss, bat at the white eyelet dust ruffle.

"Nij? Come on, kitty, kitty."

Nijinska spat again and swatted the dust ruffle, claws aggressively extended.

"What is *that* about? Come on, Battle Cat, I want to go to sleep."

Katy grabbed the cat by the scruff of the neck, and hauled her onto the bed, then peered cautiously under the dust ruffle just in case there really was something--a mouse, for instance-- under the bed.

All Katy saw was a sheet of paper--that odd old page that her mother claimed had fallen out of her dance bag. As she retrieved it, Nijinska fled into the bathroom, mewing.

"There it is! I wondered where..."

It *seemed* to be the same yellow, crumbly sheet of paper. But the words written in the spidery handwriting were not the words she had read yesterday morning. The page Katy held in her hand read

28 August
Padua, Italy
I cannot puzzle out what hold the girl has on me. After near a week of sitting in that cursed stinking studio to watch her, today I made myself a fool. I only pray I was not observed.

I resolved on awakening that I would not go near the studio today, but would instead pass a pleasant afternoon in the company of friends. In spite of this determination, the afternoon found me inexplicably standing before the very door I had vowed to eschew! Worse, I did not enter it, but, at the mercy of some ungovernable compulsion, I secreted myself in the filthy, rat-infested alleyway beside the butcher's and waited.

As the sun lowered westerly, I spied the girl as she left the sculptor's and, like the lowest sneak-thief or pick-pocket, I crept behind her through the market streets and followed her.

She is a child of the Roma, gypsies living in a tribe of perhaps fifty encamped on the outskirts of Padua. Feeling myself absurd, but no longer in control of my limbs, I squatted like a common voyeur in the undergrowth of the woods around the camp and spied on her.

When she came into the camp she was caught up roughly by a mean-visaged man who might have been her father. He shook her by the arm until she handed over to him the coin she had been paid as her day's wage, and then he pushed her off to join with the other females.

I watched as she helped prepare the food for the camp. I watched as she gulped down her own small bowl of thin stew. I followed her to the creek behind the camp where she scrubbed out bowls and kettle. I knew not at all what I hoped to gain or discover by this ridiculous behavior. I knew only that I could not command my legs to take me hence.

In our absence, the man who might be her father had brought out a violin, and another had taken up a rough wooden flute. Singly and in pairs, the Roma had begun to dance. Hearing the music call her through the woods, the child dashed back toward the camp, dropping bowls from her over-loaded arms, which she was obliged to go back and recover.

Arriving at the Romani wagons, having tossed her burden of pot and bowls into one of the *wagonbeds, she gave a glad cry and leapt into the swirling circle of dancing bodies.*

She danced like the flames of the fire, like the sea dances against the cliffs, like aspen leaves dance in a wind storm. Free under the stars, she was lifted out of her mean, dirty, hungry life by the wild song of the violin and the powerful, swirling, hypnotic movements of her own body.

Perhaps this was what I had debased myself in order to glimpse, this transformation of body into spirit. I watched her from the darkness and was lost.

When the gypsies fell asleep, some by the fire, some crawling onto piles of rags in the wagons, I wrested myself back from my trance and returned to my rented house.

As I write this, it is nearing dawn. I have paced for hours among my sculptures, which now seem to me cold and dead. Bewildered, enraged, exhausted by the child's spell, I am unable to close my eyes without seeing her.

Before she fell asleep on a pallet under her wagon, the mean-visaged man called her to bring him a drink. The name he called was "Galina." I whisper it to the coming dawn like a prayer. Galina... Galina... Save me, Galina...

Through her bedroom window Katy watched the full moon (the original one) as it slowly crossed the sky. She waited a long time to fall asleep.

Chapter 9:

Snowflakes in September

Katy's first *Nutcracker* rehearsal was called for
the following Monday at the old Opera House
where the show would also be performed.   The
Opera House had been constructed in the mid-
1800's, had fallen into disuse and disrepair after
the decline of vaudeville, and had been lovingly
restored in the early-1990's.

The seats were green velvet, the railings were
all lavishly carved and gold-leafed, the walls were
covered with fabulous painted murals, and even
the carpets had been specially woven in England
to reproduce exactly the pattern of the original
19th century floor coverings.   The city was
justifiably   proud   of   it's   richly   ornamented
auditorium; it was a beautiful little jewel-box of a
performance hall.

Unfortunately, by the time the auditorium
had been completed, the Citizens' Committee to
Restore the Opera House (CCROH) had run short

of money, leaving the rehearsal studios and the shop areas to fend for themselves. The studios were in fairly good shape, bare and utilitarian in comparison with the gorgeous crystal-chandeliered lobby below them, marred by a few cracks in the plaster and some peeling paint, but in reasonably sound condition.

In the basement, however, lurked the secret, shameful failure of CCROH: the disgraceful wreckage of the scenery and costume shops. They were a moldy, dilapidated wreck, but they were also the essential plot point in an annual drama acted out between the city council and the technicians who worked in them.

Every year the scene builders and the stagehands threatened to quit if the shops weren't improved. Every year the city council agreed to give them more money if they would stay, a much cheaper and easier solution than remodeling the basement. After five or six years of this, the technicians now enjoyed handsome salaries, and the city council no longer worried about their decaying property. It had proved to be a highly satisfactory arrangement for everyone.

Monday afternoon after school, as Katy climbed the creaky back stairs of the Opera House to the third floor studios for the first rehearsal of "Waltz of the Snowflakes," her stomach was almost as jumpy as it had been at the audition.

This was her fourth *Nutcracker*. Four times she had been chosen from huge groups of dancers as one of the city's best in her age group. Four times she had stood just outside the rehearsal hall door thinking, *This time they're going to find out that I really can't dance.* For the fourth time she took a deep breath and went in anyway.

She entered the rehearsal hall a little diffidently, unnoticed (or just unacknowl-edged) by the fourteen older girls who were putting on their pointe shoes and doing their preliminary relevés at the barre.   They were all advanced students, strong on pointe and aged between fifteen and seventeen; they seemed larger than life to Katy, and their easy control as they fooled around on pointe made her sigh and wonder if she would ever have that degree of strength and control in her feet.   They, she was certain, were feeling the floor at this very moment.

.   Katy slipped into the corner where the four other dancers Katy's age were huddled, all trying not to look either too intimidated or too presumptuous. She didn't know any of them, but they smiled at her timidly.

"Hi. This is the 'Snow' rehearsal, right?"

A chorus of soft yeah's greeted her.

"I'm   Katy.   Are   you   guys   the   other Attendants?"

"They are.   I'm just the understudy.   I'm Robin. This is Leah and Stephanie and Kim."

Katy remembered Leah and Kim from the audition; they were both excellent dancers. Maybe the Attendants would have more to do this year.

"You're understudy for Clara, too, aren't you?" asked the girl introduced as Stephanie.   Katy nodded.   "Okay," said Robin, "I guess I should learn your position first.   When do you dance Clara?"

As a "floating" understudy for all four dancers, Robin's job was to learn the part of each of them well enough to step in at a moment's notice and replace them--with no collisions, no hesitation, nothing that would let the audience identify an unfamiliar presence in the tightly coordinated group.   And she would have to learn it while standing at the back of the room, out of the way of

the rest of the cast, moving discreetly enough not
to distract the eye of the director from the "real"
dancers. If one of them was absent, Robin could
rehearse in her place, but that might never
happen. She'd be lucky to get even one full-out
rehearsal before she replaced Katy on-stage. And
of course, Katy was in the same position as
Brianna's understudy.

Katy sat on the floor and dug through her
dance bag for her slippers. "I don't do Clara till
the last Saturday matinee," she told Robin.
"There's no special rush."

"Have they said who's dancing Snow King?"
Leah asked.

"Some guy from New York," replied Stephanie,
"but... Oh no! My elastic broke. Anybody got a
safety pin I can borrow?"

"I've got a needle," volunteered Kim. "Want
me to sew it for you?"

"Oh I can do it," Stephanie sighed. "I just
hate sewing shoes." She took the needle and
thread and went to work on her slipper. "Anyway,
the guy from New York isn't in town yet," she
continued. "So I guess they won't rehearse with
us until later. Lise Moreau is doing Snow Queen.
She's so gorgeous!"

"That's what's on the cast list," Leah
whispered conspiratorially, "but did you get a look
at her at the audition? She looked like she didn't
know where she *was* even!"

"Maybe she was sick," offered Robin. "Hey!"
she chirped brightly, "I could understudy *her*!
That I wouldn't mind doing!"

Kim laughed. "If Lise Moreau can't dance, a
dozen Snowflakes will be all knocking each other
down trying to get into her costume. And whoever
wins, she'll have two understudies doing the exact
same thing trying to get *her* part!"

"Excuse me, ladies," called a pleasant female voice, "if I could have your attention for a moment."

Katy looked up, delighted to see Tanya Quint, the genial pixie who had taught their audition. "I have a couple of announcements to make before we begin."

The room became quiet and still.

"Just so you'll know, there will be no formal warm-up given before we start rehearsals. If you would like to come early and give yourself a barre, you may use the long hallway at the top of the stairs. There are a few portable barres there already. We'll try to have more by next week..."

Tanya (as she invited them to call her) read quickly through a short list of similar announcements, and the rehearsal began. As rehearsal mistress, Tanya was responsible for knowing--well enough to teach and polish--Hugh Langford's choreography for the entire two-hour ballet. Every note. Every part. Every step. She was a five-foot-tall walking dance computer with corn-rowed hair and a nice laugh.

For a long while Katy and the other Attendants had nothing to do but sit as far out of the way as possible and watch while the older dancers worked. Tanya began by demonstrating a short series of steps, first very slowly, then gradually up to tempo, and finally with the music. When the group had memorized one sequence, Tanya added another, until perhaps fifteen seconds of dance had been taught.

Once the individual dancers had memorized their steps, small groups of dancers were interlaced into braids of moving bodies, criss-crossing in intricate patterns of turns and leaps across the floor.

It did, in fact, have some of the same hypnotic effect of falling snow, except for the occasional abrupt near-collision when a dancer would misjudge or misremember her assigned pattern. But then Tanya would laugh, the needed correction would be given, and the sequence repeated.

At this level, the dancers learned quickly, so the steps accumulated rapidly, and the understudies were already looking a little confused and worried.

After Tanya had stuffed the older dancers full of as many steps as they could retain for the day, and had soothed the panic-stricken understudies, assuring them that they *would* be able to memorize all the parts, she motioned Katy's group forward and began to work with them.

"Ok, now some of this will probably change," she said. "So don't get too attached to it. But we'll start with a run in from the corner."

Katy groaned inwardly. For some reason, stupid as it seemed, running was one of the things she found hardest to do gracefully. You had to stay high on your feet without really tip-toeing, lead with your toes pointing instead of your heel flexing, stretch your legs way out in front of your upper body as you ran, and usually do something slow and smooth with your arms while your feet were going a million miles a minute underneath you. Katy had never done it right one time in her whole life. She always felt like the Frankenstein monster trying to waltz, and she suspected that she looked pretty much that way, too.

The other girls obviously felt the same, because they exchanged glances on the way to the corner. But they lined up and began their runs, Tanya leading, showing them the speed and the arm movement she wanted, and they followed behind her like awkward baby ducks waddling after their mother.

Then Tanya sat down and watched them do it on their own several times, calling corrections as they crossed the long diagonal. After four or five tries she stopped them and let them catch their breath.

"Well..." she shrugged noncommittally, "we'll work on it. Okay, next step..."

By 6:00 the rehearsal was over and the 19 sweaty, brain-dead dancers began gathering up their belongings, pulling on sweatpants, and dribbling out into the hallway.

"Whoah! What's this?" Stephanie laughed. The hallway was packed with boys, aged perhaps eight to fourteen. There were ten of them, but they were rowdy enough for fifty.

"Toy Soldiers," Leah explained as she waved to one of the boys. "That one's my stupid brother," she added, wrinkling her nose scornfully.

The Soldiers were the catch-all part for boys who could dance at least a little, but who weren't exactly young Baryshnikovs. They were all a little hyper at being in an all-boy rehearsal, instead of an all-girl classroom.

Serious young male dancers take men's classes in summer workshops, where they begin to learn the huge floating jumps and other power steps that female dancers generally don't do. But only in the largest professional schools are men's classes available year-round. And not until their mid-to-late teen years, when their upper body strength is more developed, do they begin partnering classes, where they work on the difficult and sometimes dangerous lifts required for classical pas de deux. Until then, a boy who wanted to dance was usually doomed to be the

lone male in a female world. It wasn't a
comfortable arrangement, and not many young
men had strong enough self-concepts to deal with
it.

So an all-male rehearsal was a treat, and the
young artists were rough-housing a little in the
hall, shoving playfully into each other, staging
imaginary battles with invisible swords,
experimenting with elaborate stage-combat
techniques loosely adapted from martial arts
films. Katy saw Stephanie and Leah roll their
eyes at each other as they threaded their way
through the young warriors toward the stairway.

Katy's eye was drawn by the oddly familiar
face of a dark-complexioned boy sitting alone by
the stairwell door pulling on his shoes. There was
nothing unusual about him. He wore the standard
dress-code attire of black tights and white T-shirt.
His black hair was very short and stood straight
up in a slightly spikey brush-cut. Katy just
couldn't quite place him. She pulled open the
heavy door to the stairwell to follow Stephanie and
Leah down to the parking lot.

At that moment the boy looked up and caught
Katy's eye. He looked down immediately, but too
late. Katy recognized those dark almond eyes
now. In her mind's eye she saw a tiny muscular
figure marching bravely up to a adjudicators' table
to thank the people who had just eliminated her
from an audition. An overheard name bubbled up
from her memory. "Samantha?" she whispered.

Chapter 10:

Sam

The "boy" looked up in horror.

Katy dropped her dance bag and scrunched down beside the little impostor. "You were at the audition, weren't you? You were the one who came back after cuts to thank the judges."

Samantha swallowed hard and glanced around nervously. "Oh man! Are you gonna tell?" she asked Katy anxiously.

"Don't be ridiculous," Katy said. "But how...?"

"Ummm... I went to the boys' audition."

"You *what*?!?"

Samantha looked around again, but none of the other Soldiers were within hearing distance.

"See, after I got cut, I had to call my mom to pick me up and then wait in the lobby until she came," Samantha said, "and I heard one of the moms ask at the registration desk what time the boy's audition was, and that gave me the idea. It was right after ours, but I still had a couple of hours, so I got Mom to drop me off at one of those no-appointment haircut places, and I sent her to buy me a white T-shirt and black tights. Oh yeah--and a dance belt," Sam giggled as Katy gaped in amazement. "Boy are *those* uncomfortable!

"Then I showed up back at the college and registered as 'Sam' Mia. The rest, as they say, is history."

"That... that is *so* cool!" Katy whispered. It was exactly the sort of thing that Katy could never have done in a million years, and the outrageousness of it filled her with admiration.

"So you won't tell, will you?"

"Of course not."

"Thanks," Samantha said earnestly. "This is really important to me. I told my mom that I'm going to change dance schools after Christmas, but it'll take me *so* long to catch up with guys like you who started out in a good school. And in the meantime, I figure I can learn a lot from doing this show."

Tanya appeared at the studio door, and whistled shrilly. "Let's go, gentlemen!" She pointed sternly toward the studio, and the unruly group of boys untangled themselves and started moving into the studio.

"Uh-oh," Samantha said. "Gotta go. Thanks again, uh... what's your name?"

"Katy. Katy Moon. And you're welcome. I think it's a riot. Good luck."

The two grinned at each other a second, then "Sam" slung her dance bag over her shoulder and swaggered into the studio. On the way in, one of the other boys stuck out a hand to introduce himself, and Samantha shook it with a casual, masculine gesture, laughing easily with the boy as they entered the studio.

"Amazing," Katy muttered. "I am *so* impressed." And she headed down the stairwell.

Katy was now the only dancer on the stairs. Her talk with "Sam" had delayed her until everyone else had left. The stairwell was one of those closed-in affairs with doors that open onto each floor as you come to it. It was a little confusing, since the doors were not numbered, and there was even an extra half-floor, the mezzanine, which was sort of a balcony area looking down on the lobby.

Either because of that, or because she was preoccupied with thoughts of Sam's outrageous fraud (or perhaps for some less pedestrian reason), when Katy stepped through the door that should have led to the backstage entrance and out to the parking lot, she found herself instead stepping into the basement shop area. The door clicked shut behind her.

She stood still for a moment, frowning in confusion. When she realized that she must have just gone down one flight too many, she turned around to retrace her steps, reached for the door handle, and encountered... nothing. No handle. No push bar. Just a sign that said, "This door must remain closed at all times."

"Well, no problem," she muttered, her mouth twisted in an irritated smile. She turned around to face the basement.

Being stuck in the shop didn't particularly bother her. Katy had spent too much of her life backstage to be ill at ease in a brightly lit scenery shop.

There was an exit in plain view, a big loading dock door with a smaller door beside it; the smaller door even stood ajar. The light was dimmer in that direction, but through the open door she could clearly see the driveway that sloped down to the basement level where trucks could unload large equipment and scenery directly into the shop.

Probably people were even working down
here, although she couldn't hear anyone. She set
off across the shop floor toward the open door.

The shop was configured like a huge open
garage space with work-tables and tall shelf units
crammed full of battered paint cans, their labels
obscured by drips of every possible color. There
were peg-boards half-filled with tools where black
Marks-a-lot outlines of hammers and screwdrivers
commemorated their misplaced companions. The
wall space not occupied by tools and supplies
contained jumbled stacks of old scenery and
props: chairs from every historical period since
chairs were invented, fake doors and windows
made of styrofoam, odd cardboard columns and
pieces of "stone" wall.

The floor that Katy was crossing was marked
with ancient outlines of spray-painted flats. The
dimmer light here in the center of the space and
the strange criss-crossed paint lines made the
floor surface look uneven; she more than once
expected to find a step down where there was only
level floor.

She felt herself growing a little uneasy, not
necessarily because the place itself was
unsettling--although it was a little, with all its old
ghostly furnishings of so many imaginary lives--
but also because she was an unauthorized person
in an area clearly intended for "authorized
personnel only." It was not the sort of rule she
was comfortable breaking. Also the basement
smelled of mold and solvents and felt somehow
unhealthy. She quickened her steps.

She passed a small dark office where the red
"on" dot of a coffee pot glowed like a tiny
bloodshot eye. In the back of a locked chain-link
cage of power tools, she heard a soft scurrying
sound, like a small, secretive animal. Her heart

started to beat a little harder than she liked, but the open door was much closer now. Just a few more yards...

A door to her left swung silently open. Katy jumped and let out a little frightened squeak. The room was dark except for the dim light that spilled into it from the shop, but Katy could see what the room contained. And what she saw froze her in fear.

In the gloom stood eight young girls, perhaps 12 years of age. Each with long hair, curled and tied back from their faces with satin ribbon. Each wearing a lovely old-fashioned dress. Each staring toward Katy with unseeing eyes. Each standing in perfect, unmoving stillness.

Chapter 11:

Claras

Katy could not move or make a sound except for the hammering of her heart. She couldn't look away from the ghost-like children standing in the dark. She couldn't run. She couldn't think. She could only stand there, terrified and helpless.

She blinked. Then she laughed. Mannequins! They were mannequins! She walked to the door and flipped on the light switch. Only a feeble illumination came from the filthy light fixture on the ceiling, but it was enough to change the contents of the room from macabre to delightful. Katy knew exactly what these were now. These were the Clara costumes.

This year, to promote *The Nutcracker* performances, the Dance Council planned an exhibit of all the Clara costumes that had been used in previous *Nutcrackers* in the city, dating back almost 50 years. They would be displayed in the various malls and banks and other public places in the city as part of the publicity for the show.

Katy walked reverently around each of the eight mannequins, careful not to brush against them with her dance bag. The costumes were like wearable wedding cakes, diaphanous layers of pastel chiffon with silk flowers and satin ribbons and thousands of tiny pleats. Unable to resist, Katy reached out a hand and picked up the pale blue skirt of the costume nearest her.

Her hand felt suddenly warm, as though she had plunged it into dry sand on a sunny beach. The warmth came from the costume. It was a pleasant, friendly feeling. Welcoming. As though the lovely little dress was grateful to be touched after so long alone in the dark. Katy let her dance bag slide off her shoulder, and took another corner of skirt with her other hand.

Like a current of electricity racing through a closed circuit, Katy felt a sensation of gaiety zing through her. She knew--without knowing how she knew it--that what she felt was some trace of the young dancer who had worn this costume before Katy Moon was born.

"Jane," Katy whispered. "Your name is Jane."

She felt the dress laugh happily in agreement.

"You love to dance."

"Yes! Oh, yes!!" the dress agreed.

Katy stood holding the dress for several minutes, feeling Jane's bright presence, smiling with the sense of fun that flew like sparks from the fabric. As she finally let the skirt drop from her fingers, she felt it almost sigh with sweet regret at their parting. She turned to another dress, a pink one. She ran her hands from the shoulders down the sleeves to the delicately embroidered wrist bands. The dress responded.

"Margaret?" Katy whispered. Margaret's costume carried the imprint of a completely different personality. Harder and stronger than

Jane, more mature, more determined. As Katy held the sleeves, she could feel Margaret looking past the role of Clara, already envisioning herself as Sugar Plum and Giselle and Odette. This Clara dress was just one step up a long staircase of costumes that Margaret would wear and discard without ever looking back.

"I guess I would have admired you," Katy murmured to the dress, "but I wouldn't have liked you much. We wouldn't have been friends, would we?"

"Friends?" the dress repeated. Katy felt its puzzlement as she released the sleeves.

The third and fourth dresses were confusing jumbles of sensations. Katy had the impression that too many girls had worn them, or that the girls had somehow not imprinted themselves as powerfully as Jane and Margaret. She turned to the fifth dress.

As Katy took hold of its pale yellow pleats, she felt a spirit that was calm and quiet, patient and dutiful. Katy felt the sweetness of a gentle child trying hard to please. There was also a melancholy underneath, a sad certainty that even her most earnest efforts were doomed to failure. Katy recognized these feelings immediately. They were as familiar to her as her own image in the mirror.

Katy instinctively reached in with her mind to comfort the sad spirit, but as she did, she felt with horror that the dress had also taken hold of *her*. The feeling that ran through her body now called wordlessly to her with hope, with longing, with a deep loneliness that clutched at the possibility of love.

Then in an instant it became a silent scream, shaking Katy violently. It was pain and need and some nameless terror. It crept toward Katy's heart like a cold snake, clutching at her, trying to grab hold, pleading, "Save me!! Please, please!! Save me!!"

"Lise!"   Katy half whispered, half choked. From behind her, a pair of strong hands took hold of Katy's shoulders, and the eerie grip of the costume on her mind was severed instantaneously, as though turned off like a switch.

Katy shrieked and spun around. It was Mrs. Pye.

The old woman held her until her trembling subsided, then, looking deep into her eyes, said gravely, "Katy Moon, we have to talk."

She headed off at a quick pace across the scene shop, holding Katy's hand in one of her own, lifting her long skirts with the other, tugging the girl along behind her.

With a brisk, business-like air, Mrs. Pye stepped up to a tall pile of old scenery remnants and wrestled from the stack a large styrofoam door. It was painted gold and green and had a large chunk missing from the upper right hand corner. The old woman dusted it off a bit and propped it against a bare spot of wall. "Here. This will do," she declared.

Mrs. Pye took hold of the door's styrofoam handle and pulled it, as though she were opening a real door. Katy's head began to spin.

Behind the styrofoam, where there should have been a blank expanse of basement wall, was a cozy sitting-room with a rocking chair and an overstuffed armchair arranged in front of a cheerily blazing fireplace. Between the two chairs was a small table; on the table were two lovely rose-colored china teacups with odd markings on them like Roman numerals. Only not quite.

"Come and have a cup of tea, dear. It's just made," Mrs. Pye said as she seated herself in the rocker.

Chapter 12:

I Know You, Katy Moon

Katy was too rattled to even argue about the wisdom of walking through a fake door and drinking tea inside a solid concrete wall. She dropped weakly down in the armchair, accepted the steaming cup, and sipped cautiously at it. It felt wonderfully warm going down, and unusually nourishing.

"Real cream," Mrs. Pye nodded happily. "That's the secret. Not milk. How are you feeling, dear?"

"A little, ummm... confused."

"Well I should hope so," smiled Mrs. Pye. "If you're not confused, I have serious doubts about your sanity. The Buddhists have a saying, you know," she continued, "that 'If you think this is real, you're a fool; but if you think it's not real, you're a bigger fool.'"

"Yes," Katy agreed numbly, looking around cautiously. "That seems to pretty much describe this."

Mrs. Pye was searching for something. She shook out her skirts, checked three or four pockets, looked under her teacup.

"Can I help you find something?" offered Katy.

"My spectacles, dear. Do you see them anywhere?"

"Ummm... you're wearing them."

"Ah! So I am!" Mrs. Pye chuckled, patting the little round granny-glasses which had slipped down low on her tiny nose. "How old are you, Katy?'

"Thirteen."

"And probably you've begun to notice some unusual differences between yourself and the other people around you, haven't you?"

Katy nodded.

"Things sometimes look different to you? Especially people?"

"Yes!"

"For how long? The last year? Two years?"

"I think the first time I was about four or five."

Mrs. Pye's eyes widened in surprise. She frowned and muttered, "Too young. Far too young."

"Too young for what?" Katy asked hesitantly.

"To inherit. Most Delve Novitiates are older, usually much older, before they start to experience what you have. This presents all manner of difficulties... One hardly knows how to proceed..." She seemed to be lost in thought, staring into the fire.

"Mrs. Pye?" Katy asked hesitantly. "Inherit what? And what is a Delve Whatever-you-said?"

The old woman seemed to make up her mind about something. "Quite right. Nothing to do now but grab the bull by the horns. We'll start at the beginning." She set her teacup down resolutely.

"It's a long story, Katy Moon, one that most people like yourself discover gradually over a period of years. But we haven't much time, and there are things you need to understand, so listen carefully and I'll try to tell you as much as I can quickly.

"First, some basic common-sense science. Each creature in the universe, from a one-celled organism to the most highly evolved intelligent life (which *may* be humans, I have no way of knowing, but I have some serious doubts) perceives only those pieces of the world around them that they are equipped to perceive. For instance, if an animal has no eyes, it doesn't see, right?"

Katy nodded.

"I say this so you will understand that what I'm about to explain to you is not necessarily The Big Picture. Like all other creatures, I am also limited in my understanding by my equipment. There are layers of truth, strata of reality that I can't see because I don't have the 'eyes' to see them with. But I do know some things. And these I'll tell you as truthfully as I can.

"Living beings may be categorized... " she broke off, seemingly on the verge of a giggling fit, "this sounds like a wretched zoology lecture, doesn't it? If I only had... There are some wonderful ways of explaining, if I could take you to..."

Katy touched Mrs. Pye's arm. "It's okay. I don't mind how you tell it. I just want to know."

"Of course you do, dear. Poor thing, you must be so confused..." Mrs. Pye drew herself together with a deep breath. "Very well. I'll try to be well-organized. It's not my best thing, but I'll make an effort.

"First: most plants and animals know about the world only on the basis of sensory information they receive directly from touch, sight, smell, sound, and taste. They react to these inputs and conduct their lives based exclusively on them. Let's call this group First Order Beings, or Pericepts.

"A Second Order group, the Rumin, which includes most humans and some other animals, have evolved intellectually to be self-aware, analytical, able to think about the future and the past, able to imagine what they can't directly experience.

"There is at least one more level: the Delves, the Third Order. There are probably many more levels than that, but I only have Third Order eyes, so to speak.

"Delve sight and abilities have evolved from the intuitive senses as Second Order Rumin abilities have from the perceptual. As a Delve matures, she (or he; there are some male Delves) gradually learns to burrow down to the essence of other beings, their true self, which a Delve can see as sort of diaphanous layer that lies over their physical appearance. Rather like being able to see extra colors."

Katy's head snapped up at this. Mrs. Pye looked at her carefully.

"That, too?"

Katy nodded again.

"Oh my. Quite unexpected." She seemed to become lost in her thoughts again. "Perhaps it's related to the dance training," she mused, "focusing the mind like meditation..."

"And this is an inheritance?"

"Of a sort. Most Delves have come from one of a half-dozen families, although in recent years we've seen more and more individuals develop these abilities without any family history of it it all. As though something in the human species itself might be maturing and evolving.

"Not every family member--not even every generation--produces a Delve.   And some that have the potential don't develop it.   But the abilities never quite die out of a family entirely. Every couple of generations a likely candidate emerges who usually begins to discover her abilities at about age 13 or 14. Never before," the old woman said with a slightly disapproving look, "as young as four."

"I hope I haven't made too much trouble for you," Katy offered by way of apology for her precocity.

Mrs. Pye laughed heartily, "On the contrary, my dear. The trouble has all been yours.   You should never have been left to your own devices so long. You've had no help at all through your Novitiate, poor thing.   Had we had any idea, I would certainly have looked in on you earlier. On behalf of your colleagues, I would like to extend our most sincere apologies."

"So there are really others? Like me?" Katy was astonished to feel her eyes fill with tears at the idea that she had "colleagues."

Mrs. Pye rose from the rocker and came to perch on the arm of Katy's chair, wrapping an arm around her shoulders. "So many years!" The old woman's voice trembled, and so did Katy's shoulders. "So long not to be seen and known!" She lifted Katy's chin to look into her eyes. "Well, *I* see you, Katy Moon. And I *know* you. Who you are--what you are--is not hidden from me."

It took several moments for Katy to control her tears of relief. Mrs. Pye produced a needed tissue, and as she blew her nose, a thought nagged her.

"Mrs. Pye?   At the audition?   Mr. Langford really frightened me. Is he a Delve?"

Mrs. Pye shook her head. "Hugh Langford is a creature apart. Not Delvish, no, but something... separate. A Rumin who has been altered, mutated somehow. He is frightening. And he is dangerous. As Lise Moreau discovered too late to escape him. I don't know everything there is to know about Hugh Langford. But I'm afraid I shall soon know much more than I wish to. We've not done with each other, he and I." The old woman looked grim at the thought.

"But what is he then?"

The old woman held up a cautionary hand, listening to something that Katy could not hear, something that disturbed her. She stood up quickly from the arm of Katy's chair and pulled Katy to her feet. "I think you need to go dear. You've been missed."

"Oh. All right... Should I...?"

Mrs. Pye opened the door and propelled Katy through it and back into the scene shop. "I can't come with you, Katy. Go quickly. Straight out the back door. Don't stop, all right? Go now. I'll see you again soon."

"But Mr. Langford..." Katy insisted.

"Don't speak with him when I'm not there!" Mrs. Pye warned. She reached for the edge of the styrofoam door. "It's his voice. You're not yet strong enough to withstand his voice."

Mrs. Pye waved at her and let the "real/unreal" door close between them. Katy looked back at it. It was just a painted piece of styrofoam with a corner missing, propped crookedly against a solid concrete wall. No sitting room, no fireplace, no rose-colored teacups. And no old lady in silk patches. Just a lingering scent of nutmeg.

Katy started for the open loading-dock door, then remembered her dance bag. She had left it in the room with the mannequins.

Walking carefully to avoid touching the dresses, she eased into the room and picked up her bag. As she turned again to leave, a dark form filled the door, blocking her path.

Not Mrs. Pye this time. Hugh Langford.

Chapter 13:

Lost and Found

"Katy? Are you all right?" He bent down to her, looking into her eyes with concern.

Katy caught her breath in short gasps, not knowing whether to run from him or not. She nodded her head, yes, and tried to make some explanation of why she was there, but she couldn't seem to piece together the sentences. Finally she managed to gasp out, "I'm sorry. I came out the wrong door and was trying to get out and the mannequins were there..."

He looked over her shoulder at the mannequins and said, "Ah! Those awful dolls! They frightened you, didn't they? I'm not surprised. They would give anyone nightmares, coming on them in the dark like this."

He smiled at her encouragingly, and she couldn't help but return the smile. "Lucky I came down here. Your mother is waiting for you, and everyone was starting to get a little worried about where you were, so I thought I'd come check down here. It's easy to get turned around in a theater and find yourself someplace you don't want to be."

He took her dance bag from her, and led the way back out into the shop, closing the door behind him and locking it with a key. "It seems that each time we meet, you have a bad fright," he laughed. "At least this time instead of being the idiot who throws you eight feet in the air without warning, I can be the white knight who rescues the lovely maiden from the dungeon--a role I much prefer."

Katy beamed at the word "lovely." "I'm sorry," she apologized. "I'm not really so easily frightened. I hope you don't think..."

Hugh Langford waved away her concern with a movie-star grin that melted Katy's heart. He put her dance bag on his own shoulder and offered her his arm in the sort of gallant gesture that can only be effectively made by a dancer. "May I escort you to your car, Miss Moon?"

Katy grinned back and took his arm, allowing him to lead her back across the shop to the door she had come in. This time, below the sign reading "This door must remain closed at all times," there was a perfectly normal doorknob which opened in a perfectly normal way.

"What...?" Katy muttered. She almost remembered something. Something about the doorknob... "I thought..."

"Excuse me?" Hugh Langford said, peering down into her face.

The thought eluded her. "Nothing," Katy said. "Just muttering."

"Something I do constantly," Langford laughed. "I keep trying to convince people that it's a mark of genius. No one has believed me yet. Ah! There's your lovely mother," he said as they reached the door to the parking lot. He opened the car door for Katy and handed her her dance bag. "Here you are, Mrs. Moon. I am hand-delivering your lovely daughter."

"Why thank you, sir," Rebecca flirted. "Did she do all right in rehearsal?"

"Unfortunately, I was not there, but I'm sure she did. She is... a most extraordinary child."

"Why, thank you! We think so," Rebecca replied with a coquettish tilt of her head. Katy reddened with pleasure.

He waved cheerily, sending them on her way.

Katy wondered briefly why she had imagined him as some sort of monster. He was really very nice. Normal. And nice. Sometimes she seemed to get the weirdest ideas...

As the car pulled out of the parking lot, Katy squinted a little at the window on her side of the car. It contained an odd reflection. As though writing were being projected onto it. She extended her hand to see whether it interrupted a beam of light. It didn't.

The now-familiar spidery script simply floated on the surface of the glass, its image originating from nowhere.

ॐ

25 August
Padua, Italy

For the ten days since I first beheld Galina, I have been in torment. Tonight I shall have peace.

Three more days I lay in wait for her outside the sculptor's. Three more evenings I watched her from the woods, following her at a little distance when she wandered from the camp to gather water or wood. Three more sleepless nights I paced these rooms, collapsing as dawn arrived into feverish dreams of a dancing child.

On the fifth day, I waited in my accustomed alley in the company of my now familiar friends, the rats, for her to leave the studio, but the sun lowered, the vendors went home to their suppers, and she did not appear.

As it grew dark, I flew into a panic, ran up the worn wooden stairs, and flung open the door with a crash.   The sculptor, alarmed by my wild-eyed intrusion, rose from the simple meal he was eating. As I angrily demanded to know where the child was, he bowed repeatedly and stammered that she no longer came, that the modeling was finished, and if I should like to see the piece before it was cast...

I did not stay to reply, but raced down the steps and toward the encampment, my cape flying out behind me through the empty streets of the town.

Where the Roma had been, the woods, too, were empty except for small, secretive night creatures; silent save for the wind in the trees.   In the center of the clearing where only the marks of the wagon wheels remained in the dirt, I stood turning in desperate circles, until finally I threw myself down into the cold ashes of the campfire, screaming in despair.

I heard a stealthy noise from behind me, and turning my head, I saw a wizened, toothless old woman creep from out the woods, clutching the hand of Galina, who struggled, trying to break free of her grasp and flee back into the forest.   The crone wore a malevolent smile as she thrust the girl toward me and named her price.

From my purse, I drew out with shaking hands twice the amount the old woman had named.   The exchange was made, and I half-dragged, half-

carried Galina back to my quarters where I locked her away.

As I write this, I hear her wailing in the room next mine. It is an animal sound, lost and terrified. She has refused food and drink.

A day--two at most--and she will tire of this game and take a bit of meat or a sweet. Then she will lay herself on the soft cleanness of the sheets and become accustomed, little by little, to my presence. Finally, she will dance for me.

Even with the sounds of her keening in my ears, I shall sleep well tonight.

ह

As Katy finished reading, the letters faded away, replaced briefly by an image of Mrs. Pye sitting in a rocker, sipping her tea and peering over the tops of her little round granny-glasses. That image also faded, but Katy was nagged by something about the eyes...

Katy remembered. Mrs. Pye's eyebrows turned up at the corners. Like Spock's. Or an elf's. Or Katy's.

Chapter 14:

You Can Weed My Book

Saturday morning Katy sat at the breakfast table with Nijinska on her lap, a convenient arrangement for them both because it allowed Katy to covertly re-deploy the portions of her breakfast that she didn't want (which was most of it) and still keep the cat out of Rebecca Moon's line of sight as she bustled around the kitchen. In the sentimental after-glow of Katy's birth, Rebecca had allowed Michael to add Nijinska to the household, and she had deeply regretted it ever since. Cats ranked just below shower mildew on Rebecca's list of desirable things to have around the house.

Lately the old cat had been much more affectionate than usual, and always seemed to be nervous and whiney unless she was in physical contact with the Moon-child. Nijinska's intuition operated on the basis of vaguely-perceived signals in the air around her; what she tasted in the air these days left her anxious and worried. More and more often she would reach up with a paw and pat Katy's cheek, reassuring herself that the Moon-child was close and unharmed.

"Kady?" Two pairs of identical gray eyes appeared just above the edge of the table. Above the eyes were two wildly tangled mops of long red-gold hair, and below the eyes twenty fat fingers gripped the tabletop.

Katy smiled. Most days the twins were too cute to be annoying. "Hi, guys. Want some breakfast?"

Alexis grinned and nodded, making the big rat's nest in her as-yet-uncombed hair bobble back and forth. She circled around to one side of her big sister's chair. Silent, solemn-eyed Abigail took the other side, and the two tiny mooches cuddled up to Katy while she fed them small bites of bread and strawberry jam, which Nijinska wouldn't touch.

After three bites, Abby stopped eating, although Alix continued. Abby reached up with small jam-sticky fingers and softy patted Katy's cheek, a gesture remarkably similar to Nijinska's. The usually silent twin whispered, "Don' be sad, my Kady."

"I'm not sad, baby," Katy smiled back. But it wasn't true.

For five days, ever since the events in the scene shop, Katy had wanted to talk to someone--anyone--about the things that were happening to her. The fact that there *was* no one she could talk to had left her deeply depressed.

Her mother was completely out of the question. Rebecca Moon was a very busy woman, and it wasn't easy to catch her at a time when she wasn't rushing off to a committee meeting or chauffeuring her daughters to an activity.

More importantly, her mother was not someone for whom the mysterious held any appeal at all. Faced with an account that smacked of the supernatural, Rebecca was much more likely to whisk you off to the doctor for a psychological make-over and a good dose of anti-depressant medication than to hold your hand and marvel with you at the unseen forces of the universe.

Her father, Katy suspected, might actually be approachable, even about something like this. But her father was hardly ever home before Katy went to bed, and when he was, he was still working.

Katy had a fair number of friends at the Conservatory, but none to whom she could entrust this sort of bizarre confession. And at school, like a lot of serious dance students, she operated more or less on the fringes of the various groups, friendly with everyone, close friends with no one.

It was not the first time that she had felt the lack of a genuinely intimate relationship, but it was, perhaps, the first time she had been desperately in need of one.

Abigail look across her big sister to Alexis and said an unprecedented second sentence of the morning. "My Kady sad."

"Cheer wup, Kady!" Alexis urged brightly, and bestowed a hug that left a big butter stain on Katy's sweatshirt. "You can weed my book," she suggested, placing her much-cherished copy of *Puss-in-Boots* in Katy's lap.

The two little faces were too earnest to resist, Abigail's concerned and serious, Alexis's cheerily confident, and Katy's return smile was genuine. "Oh, okay. For *you*, I'll cheer wup."

The twins gave her a matched set of strawberry kisses and ran off holding hands, their mother in close pursuit with a hair brush.

Maybe it's all over, Katy thought to herself as she thumbed through the familiar pages of the fairy tale. Since the weird events in the scene shop, she had been to two more rehearsals, and nothing else strange had happened.

Without warning, Nijinska reached up and clawed Katy's hand as it reached to turn the page of the book. The cat was staring at the book and growling softly.

"Ow! Nij! What the..."

On the fourth page of the book, the bright primary colors of the illustrations were interrupted by the handwritten words

1 September
Padua

Katy pushed her chair abruptly back from the table and drew back from the book with a gasp.

Finding herself suddenly dumped on the floor, Nijinska stood up on her back paws and reached a paw up to pat the Moon-child's knee, disturbed and mewing.

"Sorry, Nij," Katy murmured as she picked the cat back up. "That's getting to be really creepy."

Not wanting to touch the open book again, she stood over it and watched the words slowly emerge across the page, like a snake rising coil by coil to the surface of a dark pond.

1 September
Padua
For a week I have kept her, locked tight away in my upper room. The servants whispered among themselves at the cries they heard in the night. I have sent them away. I myself carry up to her the trays of food and return them to the kitchen untouched. For a week she has refused to eat,

refused to speak, refused absolutely--whether I beg her or beat her--to dance.

For seven days I have owned her, but I have no pleasure from her.

❧

The handwriting faded out and the well-shod Puss reappeared. Katy sat down again, holding Nijinska tightly.

"Get that cat off the table!" called Rebecca.

"She's not on the table, Mom," Katy replied automatically. "She's just in my lap."

"No animals at the table. It's nasty." Rebecca Moon was not easily distracted by legalisms. "Time to go. Alix? Abby? Get in the car!"

Nijinska was fretting, so Katy held her under one arm like a furry, deflated football while she cleared her dishes with the other hand.

"Gotta go, Nij," she murmured apologetically. "Party Scene rehearsal today. Gonna go be the-girl-who's-not-quite-as-good-as-Brianna-Wells.

"At least now we know that Mr. Langford's not going to turn into a gross slithery monster *every* time I see him. I just hate it when that happens," Katy giggles.   "It makes it *really* hard to understand the choreography. 'Now, from the corner, ladies... balancé, pas de bourrée, rrarrrgggghhhhh!' "

By the time Katy had cleared her dishes into the dishwasher, the toddlers were jacketed and mostly combed. The four of them piled into the car and headed for the Opera House.

Chapter 15:

Brianna

Rehearsals for the dreaded Party Scene had real potential for deteriorating into a free-for-all, but this one went remarkably smoothly, considering that the scene included not only dancers, but also small children and adult "civilians"--volunteer performers for whom the performing arts were pretty much unexplored territory. It was always a three-ring circus, but this year it was a well-organized one.

The three groups of participants each had their own handler. Tanya was there to direct the dancers. A slightly ditsy woman armed with games and coloring books was in charge of the small children. And the amateur adults were so intimidated by Langford that when an inattentive Party Guest pulled out his cell phone, the director's one scornfully arched eyebrow sent the device slinking back into its pocket. The staging proceeded as efficiently as could possibly be expected.

The dancers learned their sections quickly and quietly; then there was a lot of sitting and waiting while the simple pantomime sections with the rowdy children and the awkward adults were slowly beaten into submission.

During a long pause while Langford laboriously worked at getting six party guests headed in the same direction at more or less the same time, Katy found herself sitting next to Brianna.

The pretty blond squirmed uncomfortably for a few moments, then cleared her throat and said shyly, "Katy? I wanted to tell you I felt really badly when they cast me as Clara."

Katy blinked once or twice in surprise. "Why???"

"Because you were better."

Katy was so stunned that all she could do was murmur a polite denial.

"No it's true," Brianna insisted, rushing to get through her admission. "Remember when we both auditioned last year? You got Mirlitons? All I got was Party Scene. Skip in a circle. Jump up and down and clap.

"I worked hard this summer, and I think I caught up a little, but at the audition it really wasn't any contest. There were lots of girls there who were better than me, but you were the best. I don't know why they cast me at all. I was just sure I was going to get cut that last time."

"Well..." Katy stammered, grasping for some encouragement to offer, "my dad says that sometimes you get cast in a part because of acting ability or something. Maybe for Clara they wanted someone like you who had, you know, more stage presence."

Brianna shook her head sadly. "I don't even have that. My teacher watched the audition from

the gallery. She said I looked like a lump. And
that she should have sent Debra Norris to the
audition instead of me."

Brianna's enormous blue eyes filled with
tears.

"A lump??? Your teacher said *lump*???" Katy
couldn't believe it. Miss Emily wasn't always
exactly a one-woman Katy Moon fan club, but she
had never, ever called Katy anything like a lump!

Brianna nodded. "She's right. I watched you
while you did the scene with Mr. Langford. You
were wonderful. I mean I really believed you were
Clara. When I read the cast list and saw that I
had gotten the part, I thought it was a misprint. I
even made my mother call Mr. Langford and
double check. Then when I realized they had
made you my understudy, I felt so guilty! It
should have been you, Katy." Brianna looked at
Katy fearfully, as though she expected Katy to hit
her.

"It's not your fault, Brianna," Katy reassured
her. "And I'm not upset. Really. I'm really liking
doing 'Snow.' And you're going to make a
beautiful Clara. You are! And maybe you're not
as technically advanced as some people, but you
really do have sort of a special quality when you
act. I'm sure that's why they cast you."

That much was almost true. There was an
innocent vulnerability about Brianna that made
you want to take care of her, and some of it leaked
out when she danced.

Brianna looked with half-hopeful desperation
into Katy's eyes, wanting to accept the
encouragement. A moment later she gave up.

"I can't dance, Katy," she said quietly. "I can't
even do a clean single pirouette." She put her
head down onto her knees to hide her shame.
"My teacher's right. I am a lump."

Katy's arm slipped protectively around Brianna's waist. She understood in a limited way the damage done by schools like Brianna's that taught through humiliation and intimidation and by deliberately pitting one student against another, but she had no words that could help heal that damage.

As she had with the Clara costumes, Katy felt a distilled sense of the girl slowly spread up through her arm to her heart. It was similar in its feel to the Lise-self: a deep, sorrowful loneliness, a generous spirit with no place of refuge. But Brianna's sadness did not escalate into terror and pain as Lise's had, so Katy just sat quietly holding her, letting the rehearsal bustle around them.

Eventually Hugh Langford asked for everyone's attention and announced a quick review of everything that had been taught so far, promising a break afterwards "in which you may all have lunch and make your *very* important phone calls."

The dancers, the volunteer adults, and the small children all managed to stumble through their parts with only a couple of instances where children wandered off in the wrong direction or adults suddenly went slack-jawed and glassy-eyed as they forgot their instructions.

The performers drifted away to their lunch break, and Katy looked around for Brianna, intending to suggest that they eat lunch together. Her concern evaporated in a puff of jealousy as she spotted Brianna heading out the studio door, deep in conversation with Hugh Langford. He was telling her something amusing, his dark head bent low toward her neat blond bun as her blue eyes twinkled up at him.

"Humph!" Katy grumped. "I guess she *found* somebody to have lunch with." She revised her sympathy downward by about ninety percent.

"Katy Moon? Is Katy Moon still here?" came Tanya's voice from the hallway.

"Yes, ma'am, I'm here," called Katy.

Tanya had a clipboard in her hand. "Mrs. Pye needs you for a costume fitting, Katy. Do you have your lunch? Good. Take it with you."

"Where...?"

"Fourth floor. Top of the stairs." Tanya busily flipped through pages of notes as she trotted off.

At the foot of the stairs, Katy took a deep breath, set her mouth in a tight, determined line, and went up to encounter Mrs. Pye. She wasn't at all sure what she thought about the old woman's rambling fairytales about evil demon choreographers. But she did know that she preferred her rehearsals demon-free. And she had decided to tell Mrs. Pye exactly that--and also to please take her name off the list of Delvish Apprentice Sooth-seers or whatever.

At the top of the stairs, she stopped outside the door of the costume shop. From behind it she was surprised to hear what sounded like a choir humming "The Nutcracker Overture" in perfect harmony.

She opened the door, expecting to see at least six people, and was astonished to see only two: Mrs. Pye and Samantha. And Sam wasn't humming.

Chapter 16:

To See Deep and Clear

Sam was rubbing a hand through her boy-cut hair, already grinning ear-to-ear, but she managed to light up her eyes a notch brighter as Katy walked in.

"Hey, Katy! Have you heard Mrs. Pye do this humming thing? That is *so* cool!"

Mrs. Pye smiled almost shyly. "I'm polyphonic," she admitted to Katy.

"And hey! What about this Hugh Langford story? How weird is *that*?" Sam exclaimed to Katy.

Sam and Mrs. Pye were both seated at big sewing table piled high with costumes. Sam was eating an apple with her feet propped up on the table. Between them on the table was a big rose-colored sewing machine with markings on it like Roman numerals. Only not quite.

Katy looked back and forth between them in confusion. Did Mrs. Pye try to sell everybody this story? If so, the real question was why hadn't someone come to take her away in a straight jacket?

"No dear," Mrs. Pye answered the first unspoken question. "Not everybody. I asked for

Sam's assistance because of your close call last
Monday with the Clara costumes."

"It was a just little scary," Katy demurred. "It
wasn't a big deal."

"It might have become a big deal," Mrs. Pye
insisted. "It was dangerous. This time I arrived in
time to help, but next time I might not. If Hugh
Langford had walked into the shop before I did, it
might already be too late."

"But he did walk in!" Katy objected. She felt
more than a little protective of her director now,
as though he were being unfairly maligned.

"Not while you were 'connected' with Lise's
costume, dear. Had he seen that, it would have
been a catastrophe. Perhaps a fatal one."

Katy pursed her lips stubbornly. This batty
old lady was going to have to do a lot better than
this.

"So I'm your back-up," Sam grinned around a
bite of apple. "Like on *Cops*. Standard procedure
on a bust. Call for back-up before you go in."

"And you believe all this?" Katy was
exasperated now, and didn't care who knew it.

"Well," answered Sam, still chewing, but
putting her feet down and sitting up straighter,
"I'm not psychic or stuff like all you..."

"Delves," supplied Mrs. Pye helpfully.

"Right. Delves. But I do know that there is
something way creepy about Hugh Langford. And
I also know that Lise Moreau is a gorgeous
dancer, but she walks around like something out
of a vampire movie. *And* I know that while Mrs.
Pye may look like a psycho gypsy, she can do
some truly amazing stuff.   I especially like the
butterflies."

"The what?"

"You didn't see the butterflies yet?" Sam was
getting really excited now.

"Butterflies," Katy repeated flatly.

"Yeah, check it out!" Sam leaned forward across the table, staring fixedly at the rose-colored sewing machine, which just sat there, like any ordinary sewing machine, only more colorful than most.

When nothing happened, Sam looked expectantly at Mrs. Pye, who in turn was looking at Katy.

"I don't think that Katy wants to see anything more out of the ordinary just now," said Mrs. Pye quietly. "Am I right, dear?"

Katy stood very still and silent. She definitely did *not* want to see anything more out of the ordinary, but telling people "no" was next to impossible for her, even when telling them "yes" meant all kinds of unwanted complications.

"It's all right, Katy," Mrs. Pye said. "It seems a heavy burden. I'm not surprised that you're reluctant to pick it up."

Katy was again very close to tears. Sam might be enchanted with everything Mrs. Pye had told her, but what Katy wanted more than anything was to go back to her regular, non-magical everyday life exactly the way it was two weeks and a day ago. Before meeting Mrs. Pye. Before being haunted by that stupid journal. Before touching the Clara costumes. Before seeing "into" Hugh Langford.

"Maybe," Katy said with more stubborness than usual, "maybe you need to explain to me why you think Mr. Langford is so dangerous. Because I don't. I know he frightened me at the audition, but then when I saw him in the basement, and today in rehearsal he was so..."

"Charming," Mrs. Pye completed.

Katy nodded miserably.

"He is. Charming and delightful. And deadly."

Katy lowered her eyes. She didn't believe it. She didn't want to actually say that poor old Mrs. Pye was about two tacos short of a combination plate, but that's what she thought.

"Harm is not always obvious, Katy Moon. It can be subtle, and it can be slow, and it can come beautifully wrapped. Harm can be convincing you that something is for your own good when it's not at all. Harm can be making you doubt your own abilities or your own judgment about good and evil. Harm can be a slow, insidious process of convincing you to trust someone who is not trustworthy."

Katy nodded reluctantly. Something in the old woman's words felt true.

"I will tell you what I know about Hugh Langford," said Mrs. Pye. "But you must judge for yourself what is true. You have the ability to see deep and clear, if you decide to, both into my heart and into his. You can be tricked, but only if you wish to be.

"I warn you: this is a time to be stern and strong and to look truth squarely in the face, whether you like the sight of it or not. Much depends on it."

As Katy stared into those sky blue eyes, Mrs. Pye no longer seemed like a sweet, slightly befuddled grandmother. She seemed ancient and powerful, someone--or some*thing*-- that existed on a plane much different than Katy's world of school and dance class and family. Katy could not yet grasp all that Mrs. Pye was or was capable of. But she did know with absolute finality that this being before her was incapable of deceit or evil.

"All right," Katy said calmly. "Tell me what you know."

Chapter 17:

The Acquisitor

Mrs. Pye spoke quietly. "Hugh Langford was once just a man who loved beautiful things. There are people, Katy Moon, who are at their core Acquisitors. They acquire things. Their lives are spent grasping at items to add to their collections. Some collect perfectly innocent things like spoons or stamps, some collect money, some power. For the most part they are relatively harmless, as Hugh Langford was once, but in a few, their need to *own* takes over their minds and their lives and does great damage.

"Many, many years ago Hugh Langford became one of these obsessed creatures. He collected beauty. Early in his long life (for he is older--much older--than he looks) he collected beautiful pieces of intricately carved jewelry. Then paintings. Then sculptures. But it was when he began to collect human beings, young dancers, that he made himself into a monster.

"He found a way, I have never discovered how, to acquire a human being--always a young girl, and always a dancer--acquire her so completely that he *extends* himself somehow. He divests her of some part of her youth and vitality and adds it to his own.

"He has learned much. He has immense charm and wealth and authentic genius as a teacher and choreographer. He lays his abilities at the feet of his victims in exchange for what he takes from them. He can do what he promises: he can raise the level of their artistry far above what they could achieve without him.

"He is the perfect predator; his victims vie with each other for the privilege of being destroyed by him.

"He collects them now as he once did his marble and bronze sculptures. He finds them when they are between ten and fourteen years of age. He inspires them. He trains them. They dance only for him. They are allowed no life or hope or judgment or happiness outside his ownership.

"And gradually, they die inside, their minds and spirits never allowed to grow into whole selves, their life force stolen to expand his own."

"Lise Moreau," whispered Katy.

Mrs. Pye nodded sadly. "Since she was ten years old, she has been his 'student.' She came to him because she was a lonely child who wanted to dance and to be loved. She thought he was the answer to both dreams."

"What will happen to her?" Katy asked.

"Dancers are not marble sculptures," Mrs. Pye said. "They do not stay forever young. You or I would look at Lise Moreau and say that she is still beautiful, at the peak of her career. Not as strong, perhaps, as she was at seventeen, yet with an interpretive depth and finesse that a younger woman cannot match.

"But in Hugh Langford's eyes she has grown old. Worse, he has drained her now of everything that feeds him. He will discard her. And because she has never learned to exist apart from him, like her predecessors, she will be destroyed.

"I know the fates of three victims; there may have been more. Two of them died within a year after he abandoned   them.   One sank into madness. I found none that have recovered.

"Lise   Moreau   is   no   longer   capable   of sustaining him, and he is becoming desperate to replace her with another acquisition, his next work of art. Unfortunately, the item that caught his eye at the audition was the work-in-progress called Katy Moon."

Katy swallowed hard. Sam reached over and took her hand.

"It was in fear of that," Mrs. Pye continued, "that I stood at the window during your audition. What you saw then was a challenge being issued. A challenge that I made a bit prematurely, I'm afraid. He is much stronger than I realized, and I was nearly unequal to it."

"What did you do?"

"I went to war with Hugh Langford. He was about to give you your heart's desire, Katy. He had cast you as Clara. By the time the curtain went up for your first performance, you were to be his new student. And his next victim.

"For four days we struggled. I tried to defeat him once and forever in a battle of will and strength, and I failed.

"The only remedy left me was to call upon the community of Delves to protect you, and this they were able to do together.

"Tuesday night when you went to bed, your name was written as Clara on all the cast lists sent to all the schools.   Before the sun rose Wednesday morning, your name was gone, and it was not possible for Langford or any other human to write your name into that space again. He was forced to substitute another, and he chose Brianna.   He is furious, but for the moment he can do nothing more."

"But now will Brianna...?"

Mrs. Pye sighed sadly. "I will do my best to save her, Katy, but I'm not sure I have the strength left. It was a terrible thing to send any child into that trap. I did not do it willingly, but I had little choice.   I was unable to defeat him completely, and it was crucial--more so than I can tell you--that you not fall under his power."

Katy stood up abruptly and backed away from her, horrified by this admission that another girl had been sacrificed to spare her.   She wrapped her arms around herself and stood shivering. "But, Mrs. Pye, I can't let Brianna..."

The old woman held up a hand. "Katy, let me explain. This was not a question of my preferring one of you over the other.   It was not even a matter of my wishing to save 'one of my own kind.' There was more at stake here than the life of a single girl.

"By stealing the lives from these children, he has become enormously powerful. He has become unnaturally old without aging. He has become almost   irresistibly   charismatic.   You   felt   his attraction at the audition.   Even you, who were able to glimpse what he is when I appeared at the window and his attention faltered--even you came under the spell. You can again, even now, if he wishes it. If you are unwary.

"He has a skill with his voice that few can withstand. And if he charms you into an alliance with him, he will take from you not just the normal life-force of a young girl on the brink of womanhood, but all the potential of a Delve Novitiate to add to his own power. This would make him unimaginably strong--an horrific force unleashed into the world.

"I will save Brianna if I can," Mrs. Pye assured her solemnly. "I promise you this. But at all costs we must keep you from him.

"What has saved you so far, Katy Moon, is that Hugh Langford does not yet know what you are. A girl of your age with such ability is outside his experience. Even at the audition, when he saw me in the window--really saw me, as I exist in the Delve Stratum--he did not understand that you saw me, too. Or that you saw him as well. This is a secret that you must keep from him for as long as you can."

Sam was listening to this intently. "Okay," she said, "but if all this is true--and weird as it sounds, I think it is--where do I come in? Don't get me wrong. I wouldn't miss this for anything! But you guys are talking about... like... powers! Comic book superhero stuff. What Katy needs for a back-up is a Jeddi warrior. I'm just a kid with no hair."

Mrs. Pye laughed out loud. "Exactly the superpower the situation calls for," Mrs. Pye assured her. "Until Katy learns to control her own abilities, what is really needed is someone with none. And you're just the man for the job." Even Katy smiled at that.

"For instance, the costumes were a danger to her," Mrs. Pye continued. "You are a powerful seer, Katy Moon, the strongest I've met in many years in spite of your age. But you've had no one to teach you to control what you can do. This can put you at risk in a very different way. A Delve Vision that is out of your control can consume your mind, take over your thought process. It can turn from vision to hallucination. It can mean insanity.

"If Katy is caught in a vision," Mrs. Pye went on, turning back to Sam, "as she was in the basement while she held Lise Moreau's Clara costume, if you can reach her, just take hold of her hand or touch her somehow. If you can't reach her, just talk to her. Call her name. Try anyway you can to pull part of her mind back into the 'real' world. Do the same if she seems to be falling under Hugh Langford's influence. Call her back. Help her focus."

Mrs. Pye put both hands on Sam's shoulders and smiled into her eyes. "You have a brave little heart, Sam. Which is a good thing."

All three of them said in unison, "...because you're going to need it."

And they all laughed. Even Katy.

"So now check out the butterflies!" Sam insisted.

Mrs. Pye looked questioningly at Katy.

"It's really totally cool, Katy!" Sam insisted.

Katy smiled her agreement. "Sure. Why not."

Mrs. Pye sat down at the table in front of the rose-colored sewing machine. She tipped her head a little, hummed a complex phrase reminiscent of a Bach fugue, and smiled as the machine dissolved into a hundred rose-colored butterflies which rose gaily into the air, circling the three and lighting on them here and there.

"Wow!" whispered Katy.

"I *told* you!" Sam laughed. Two butterflies lit on her nose, making her go cross-eyed looking at them.

Mrs. Pye herself attracted most of the little pink things. They decorated her hair, circled her hands, and settled into her lap where they all but disappeared in her silk patches.

"Are they real?" Katy asked. A butterfly fluttered in front of her lips for a moment, "kissing" her delicately.

"Real as beans," said Mrs. Pye. "I couldn't get through the day without them. Watch." She hummed a little hum, at least three layers of harmony embedded in it. The butterflies swirled into a tornado-like funnel then seemed to be sucked down to the table where they coalesced again into a pink sewing machine.

Continuing to hum, Mrs. Pye picked up a wad of red and blue cloth and gold braid, stuffed it carelessly toward the machine, and then sat back in her chair, hands folded. The butterfly-machine seemed to grab the cloth, spread it out, and begin stitching, scraps of snipped-off fabric falling away, gold braid winding itself neatly into intricate patterns. In less than five minutes, the machine stopped. A beautifully tailored soldier costume lay beside it.

"There you go," Mrs. Pye said to Sam. "See if that fits."

To no one's surprise, it did. Perfectly.

Mrs. Pye sighed. "I'm hopeless when it comes to things like sewing. Also counting money, shoe strings, finding things... Before the butterflies came, I once spent half a day trying to figure out how to get to the kitchen from the living room."

"No kidding?" asked Sam. "Do you ever rent out a couple of them? I have this history test on Monday..."

"Sorry, dear," said Mrs. Pye. "They're sort of one-woman insects. Even for me, they won't help at all with anything I can do myself. A few years ago I figured out how buttons work, and ever since they've flatly refused to do up my blouse, even when I'm in a hurry. I suspect if you just sit down and read your assignment..."

Katy noticed for the first time that Mrs. Pye's collar was fastened a little askew, as though she had in fact put the buttons through the wrong holes. She made an unlikely Sorceress or Guardian Angel or whatever she was.

"You know," Mrs. Pye added, "The Greeks used the word 'psyche' to mean both soul and butterfly. Perhaps they're just an externalized part of me--the smarter part that can do subtraction."

One butterfly withdrew itself from the sewing machine and floated to Mrs. Pye's left hand, where it became a pocketwatch. "Quite right," Mrs. Pye nodded to the watch. "Lunch break over. Time for you to get back to rehearsal, Katy."

As the girls left the costume shop, they could hear behind them Mrs. Pye humming polyphonically to her butterflies.

"So what do you think?" Katy asked Sam guardedly.

"What's to think? She's awesome."

"But do you believe what she said about Mr. Langford and all that?"

Sam chewed on that a moment. "What I believe," she said carefully, "is that that little old lady is the real deal. I think she knows a lots of things, including some stuff that seems completely whacked out to me. But hey, lots of stuff seems that way to me. I still don't get how radios work.

"Anyway, if Mrs. Pye can show me butterflies sewing costumes, I don't see why I should argue with her about whether some creeped-out choreographer is seriously dangerous. I think I gotta give her the benefit of the doubt.

"What I *don't* get," Sam continued, "is how you can keep actually seeing with your own eyes all this weird stuff and be more skeptical about it than I am. I mean you have actual *data!*"

Katy thought that over. "Maybe," she said, "it's *because* I see things. Because all my life I've seen things that were just a little different from what everybody else saw. And I'm so used to being told that they're not really there, that I don't believe my own eyes. Or ears or whatever. You're used to seeing the same things everybody else does. You trust what you see. I don't always."

"Yeah," agreed Sam. "I guess that could make it harder. But I think you ought to at least consider the possibility that Mrs. Pye is dead right. And that you need to be very, very careful. I also think we should have each other's phone numbers. Do you have a piece of paper?"

Katy took her meticulously-maintained agenda out of her dance bag, slipped the matching pen from it's slot, and flipped to the address book; Sam scrounged around in the pocket of her jeans and came up with an old gum wrapper, unfolded it, and wrote on the back with a much-chewed stub of a pencil. As the two girls exchanged their phone numbers and addresses, they found to their surprise that they lived just four streets apart and went to the same large middle school, even though they had never had classes together.

"Convenient," said Sam. "In case of an emergency."

They reached the hallway in front of the rehearsal studio just as Tanya was herding the last stragglers back in to continue the Party Scene

staging.   Katy dashed in as Tanya gave Sam a
friendly wave and said, "Hi, Sam. How's it going?"

"Pretty good," replied Sam, waving back. "See
ya Monday."

"Bye, Sam!"   Katy sang out, grinning and
fluttering her eyelashes. "Call me, okay?"

"Uh, yeah. Bye." Sam ducked her head and
hurried off in a remarkably accurate imitation of a
13-year-old-boy embarrassed to be caught talking
to a girl.

Part Two:

Lessons

Chapter 1:

Novitiate

Over the course of the next month, Mrs. Pye instituted an informal Delve training program for Katy.   Together   they   worked   with   specific exercises to strengthen Katy's abilities and teach her control. One week she observed people sitting together in a restaurant and tried to read how they felt about each other. The next week she handled pieces of clothing and tried to control the strength of the "signal" that came from it.

Katy's ability to turn the signal on was very erratic; often she could receive nothing at all unless Mrs. Pye "boosted" the signal for her. When she did receive it, her   her ability to turn it off--or even down--was even more undependable, but Mrs. Pye insisted that progress was being made.

Katy was eager to know when she might meet other Delves, but Mrs. Pye had been vague about that, saying only that for the time being she was Katy's contact with the others, and that Katy had a lot of work to do before she was ready to join the Community.

Sam was generally included in their sessions, although after the first thrill had worn off, she declared the exercises pretty dull stuff. Katy liked them, though. They were like barre exercises for her mind. Slow, methodical, and very safe.

One bright, crisp late-October afternoon, the two girls sprawled lazily across an old-fashioned wooden park bench with wrought-iron legs, waiting for Mrs. Pye in the little ornamental park across the street from the Opera House. The three usually met there immediately after school in order to have at least an hour to work before rehearsal.

Across the park they spied Mrs. Pye tracing a circuitous path around the park lawns, deliberately walking through each pile of red and gold leaves where they had been raked for removal and composting. When she got to the biggest one, she stood with her back to it, arms straight out from her sides, fingers spread, head raised to the sky, and slowly let herself fall backwards into the heap. Katy and Sam laughed and ran to join her.

By the time they reached her she had wriggled herself deeply into the leaves and was no longer visible. "Hi, girls," the pile of leaves greeted them. "Join me?"

They did. In a very few seconds all three were deeply burrowed in autumn glory, breathing in the rich earth smell as deeply as they could for giggling. They played until Katy noticed that they were drawing the attention of a city parks worker who was clearly unhappy that his neatly raked pile was now being re-distributed.

They got up, apologetically pushed the leaves more or less back into their tidy heap, and went back to their bench. Mrs. Pye carried an inch-

worm with her on her finger which she had
rescued from a premature death under Sam's
elbow.   Mrs. Pye liberated the inch-worm onto a
bush, handed out three tuna sandwiches, and
prepared to get to work. It was time to start their
session.

This   week's   practice   involved   another
occupant   of   the   park: a   medium-sized,
nondescript dog. Katy was to try to reconstruct
without touching the dog how he had spent the
last 24 hours.

After ten minutes of watching Katy stare
fixedly at the dog, Sam was ready to wrap it up.
"But, Mrs. Pye!   It's *boring!*"   She blew on her
hands. "And it's cold! The sun's going down."

"Eat your sandwich, dear," suggested Mrs.
Pye. "Tuna is very warming. I put apples in it for
you. You can have one of my shawls if you want.
They're cozy."   For outdoor excursions, Mrs. Pye's
silk patches were swathed in a rainbow of
crocheted wool.

"It's a *dog!*" Sam objected. "We know what he
did all day.   He chased cats.   He dug through
trash cans. He chased squirrels. He dug through
more trash cans. *Nobody cares!*"

 Mrs. Pye just smiled.

Katy responded without taking her eyes off
the dog.   "Nobody cares about pliés, either, until
they have to land out of a jump," she observed.
"This could come in very handy some day."

"Only if you end up homeless and need to
know where to find a half-eaten Big Mac," Sam
sulked.

"I think I got it!" Katy spoke quietly but there
was excitement in her voice. "He spent the night
in an alley behind a cardboard box.   There's a
door in the alley to something like a restaurant--
at least there's a person in white there who gave

him scraps. Then he came to the park here and sat by someone who petted him and talked to him for a long time. There was a fight with another dog and he got bitten and it still hurts him, so he's been mostly taking it pretty easy and napping a lot today."

"Not bad, dear," approved Mrs. Pye. "The person who fed him the scraps, was it a woman or a man?"

Katy frowned in concentration. "I can't tell. It's fuzzy."

"And why is it fuzzy?"

"Because *he's a dog*!" blurted out Sam. "He doesn't *know* whether it's a man or a woman! And he doesn't care."

"No," said Katy slowly. "He does care. He likes women better than men. But there's something in the way. I can't quite see..."

Mrs. Pye whistled (monophonically), and the dog's ears went up. She whistled again, and the dog came limping over to her outstretched hand. As she scratched him under the chin, she said, "Look at his eyes, Katy."

"Oh!" Sam cried. "He has cataracts! That's what it was, Katy. He's going blind. Poor dog..." Sam was down on the ground cuddling the dog, her surliness dissolved by her pity for the elderly animal.

Mrs. Pye spoke softly. "Sam? Look at Katy."

Sam was instantly focused on her friend. Katy sat perfectly still, not touching the dog. Her pupils had dilated hugely, almost obliterating the blue of her eyes. Her breathing had become shallow. Sam touched her hand and called her gently, "Katy?"

There was no response.

"Katy? It's me, Sam... Come on back now, okay? Come back, Katy."

Gradually Katy's eyes relaxed and turned from black back to blue. She lowered her head and breathed deeply.

When she raised her head again, her eyes were filled with tears. She didn't speak. Mrs. Pye took her in her arms and held her.

"This is one of the most difficult parts, Katy: to know and care without drowning in it. The world is full of helpless beings in pain. Over and over again you will be drawn into that pain. You can't ignore it, and most of the time you can't fix it. But you also can't let yourself be overwhelmed by it."

Katy had begun to sob.

"How can she help it?" demanded Sam. "If she feels it so strongly from every person or animal around her? Can't we protect her from it somehow?" She had seen Katy incapacitated by this shared sorrow several times now, and it worried her much more than Hugh Langford, who thus far had proved completely harmless.

"No," said Mrs. Pye. "She needs to learn to handle it without protection. Katy? Listen now. There is a balance you must find between the pain and the joy. The world has great sadness in it, but also great beauty. In order to be fully awake and aware, you must learn to hold both in your heart at the same time. Look at the dog." Katy did. "Look at the totality of his experience. Tell me about it."

Katy spoke slowly. "There's pain in his hip. Confusion. He can't see and he doesn't understand why. It frightens him..."

"That's only part," prompted Mrs. Pye.

"The old woman who petted him. She had a nice smell. Like baby powder. Very gentle hands."

"What else?"

"When he slept in the sun, the warmth felt good on his hip. But there was a cool breeze that he liked.   It reminded him of running.   He dreamed of running in the woods. With another dog. A long time ago... It was fall and the woods were all yellow..." She looked up at Mrs. Pye and blinked. "His memories. They're as real to him as what happens to him right now."

"That's right, dear. That is Age's gift. He lives in the past as vividly as the present."

Katy looked at the old dog a long time. "It's still very sad, all his pain and confusion. But you're right. There's all this remembered joy, too. And contentment even now." She sighed. "It's hard."

Mrs. Pye patted her hand.   "But you're learning quickly."

Katy squirmed uncomfortably and said, "Ummm, there's something I think I should show you." She dove head down into her dance bag and came up with a spiral notebook. She flipped through it until she found a page which, instead of being blue lines filled with neatly pencilled algebra equations, was yellow and filled with a shaky handwriting and ink blots. "I, uh, got this today."

Chapter 2:

The Diary

Mrs. Pye took the journal page from her, frowning as she examined it. "What do you mean, you 'got' it? Who gave it to you?"

Katy shrugged. "Couldn't tell you. It was just there in my spiral when I opened it. It's the fifth one I've gotten. The others disappeared after I read them, so I didn't read it yet."

"You didn't tell *me!*" Sam objected.

Katy sighed. "I keep hoping if I just ignore them, they'll stop. I... I don't want to *know* these things!"

Mrs. Pye handed her back the notebook and wrapped a supportive arm around her shoulders. "Maybe you should read it aloud to us, dear," she suggested, "since clearly these are intended for you."

Katy looked uncomfortable, but she cleared her throat and read,

8 September
Padua, Italy
We have both of us descended into madness, my new possession and myself. Galina only sits clutching her knees in a corner, tears running in constant streams from her wild, blankly staring eyes.

I pace the upstairs room like a caged cat, one moment kneeling beside her to softly stroke her tangled black hair and whisper to her, the next moment screaming and striking her over and over with my riding crop.

A pretty pair: the madman and his lunatic beloved.

As the sun rose this morning, I resolved that if I could not own her, I would kill her and then myself. I drew my knife to cut her throat, but was distracted by the sound of pebbles rattling against the shutters of the barred window.   I threw open the shutters and saw on the pavement below an old crone--the same who sold me the cursed child.

She grinned toothlessly up at me, and my dagger began to shake with rage and pain in my fist.   I grabbed Galina's wrist, jerked her to her feet, and pulled her to the window, meaning to slash her throat and fling her body to the ground in front of the old woman.   I seized her by the hair and bent her backwards over the window sill, touching the blade to the tender arching curve of her neck.

The old woman called up, "Ah, but you only took away half the merchandise, my lord! You paid me for more than you got!"

I stopped my knife before it sliced more than a hair's depth into the girl's throat. I called out hoarsely, "Make her dance!"

"She only dances for love, my lord. You must make her love you."

"How?"

"Ah, that! That I will tell you. That knowledge you have already paid me for. But she has greater gifts than that. Shall I come up?"

I slammed the window closed and locked it, and in a few heartbeats, the crone was seated by the hearth in my bed chamber, sipping a bowl of broth as if she were a kinswoman invited to sup. I urgently willed her to speak, but she finished her broth first, sopping up the last with a hunk of black bread.

When she had smacked her wrinkled lips over the last taste, she winked at me and cackled, "So? She's lovely, isn't she? Such a tasty little bite of a girl. That's the age, isn't it? That sweet, fresh, ripe moment, balanced just on the lip of womanhood!"

"She must dance," I whispered. "She must dance for me."

"It's a simple matter," the old woman assured me, patting my knee. "You got the thing partly right. Kisses and kicks in equal measure. The kicks she expects, the kisses surprise her. Just you add pretty shoes and pretty tunes is all. She's a simple, stupid girl, but there's a soul to her. Bring her music that calls her aching heart. Put some soft leather on her dirty feet. She'll dance for you. She'll do whatever you want. Pretty shoes and pretty tunes is all it wants more."

My heart swelled with hope at her words. I rose to leave, my mind already at work on the task of finding cobbler and composer. The crone tugged at my shirt, leaving a dirty smudge on the silk. "There's more, my lord," she croaked. "Much more, perhaps, depending on the price you'll pay."

"What more?"

"A girl that age, she's more life in her than she needs. She's got extra portions, as it were. Extra life that can be drunk off by one who's willing to pay."

"What do you mean?"

"A man who's strong, who won't stop at a little pain, at a little sacrifice, can have that life. Can add it to his own." The black beads of her eyes were glinting in the firelight.

"You can have more than the sight of her, my lord. You can take her soul into your own, a bit at a time. She can be drunk down like a bottle of fine wine. You can own her like you own the food you ate last night and the thoughts you think this moment. Best of all, each day you take of her life, you'll save one of your own. I can show you the way."

My mind reeled at this idea. "And to bring this about...?"

The old woman stretched out her filthy old toes toward the hearth. "First steps first, my lord, the pretty shoes and the pretty tunes. Then I'll show you a thing or two that will surprise you."

Heartened at having action to take, I hurriedly repaired my wild and disheveled appearance, combing my hair and dressing in clean clothes for the first time since I brought Galina to my house.

Leaving the old woman still warming her feet by my fire, I dashed from the house to the shop of a cobbler, where I chose a piece of butter-soft crimson leather and dispatched the man back to my house to take the measure of Galina's foot.

Next I called at the homes of divers acquaintances whom I know to be patrons of musicians, not stopping, but asking at each door for the names of composers whose work they supported.

Returning to my house, again I sunk into despair at the sight of the girl. She cannot live overlong like this, starved and despairing.

The old woman assures me the solution is at hand. I will stop at nothing to save her. Nothing, that is, short of freeing her. Better that she die than exist apart from me.

ॐ

Sam spoke first. "Oh," she whispered. "Oh, Katy..."

"Do you know what these pages are, Katy?" Mrs. Pye asked softly. Katy shook her head. "But you can guess."

"They're a diary."

"Whose diary?"

"I... I don't know. There's never a name on them."

"Do you need a name, Katy? Do *you* need a signature written out?"

Katy was silent and sullen. Sam looked nervously back and forth between the two, but Mrs. Pye waited patiently. Katy became uncomfortable in the long pause and muttered, "They don't even feel like anything to me."

"The time is coming, Katy Moon, when you will have to know. What you admit to me or to Sam doesn't matter very much. But to yourself you must tell only your best and fullest truth. It is dangerous--to your body and to your soul--to do otherwise."

Katy sat looking down at the ground. She swallowed hard and said, "I think they're Hugh Langford's diaries."

"I think so, too," Mrs. Pye agreed, "though I've never seen them before."

Katy looked her square in the eyes. "So you're not the one sending them to me?"

"No, dear."

"Is... he?"

"I don't think so."

"Okay," Sam piped up, "so who is? And while we're on the subject, I have another question." Sam looked at Katy for permission to continue. Katy shrugged and nodded.

"We were talking the other night about some of the things that happened back in September. And there were some other things that happened to Katy that we didn't understand.

"Like when she couldn't get in the front door at the audition. And when the door handle in the scene shop disappeared and she got stuck down there.   And   then   the   door   to   the   Clara mannequins opened all by itself. All this door stuff. What is *that* about? Did Mr. Langford...?"

"Arrange that?"   completed Mrs. Pye. "No, dear. Nor did I. I don't know who or what did. I would guess that it's the same one who is sending Katy these pages, but honestly, I don't *know* that to be true.

"As I told you, Katy, I don't see all that there is to see. But it does seem to me that you are being guided--and rather insistently--through a series of doors into places where you will learn things you need to know. Just as you are being shown the things written in Hugh Langford's journals.   And I believe that you can trust whatever power is at work there."

Mrs. Pye smiled at Sam. "Perhaps one of those doors will open one day, and Katy will meet that power face to face. If she does, I'd like an introduction."

Katy hugged the old woman. "I'm not opening any more doors without you. You can introduce yourself."

Mrs. Pye smiled. Sam, who had already learned to watch more carefully than she used to, thought the smile was a little sad.

"Well, girls?" said Mrs. Pye, patting them both on their knees, "shouldn't you be getting into rehearsal?"

"We have twenty minutes!" Sam protested.

"I thought you were cold," Katy reminded her, standing up. "I want to go get changed and stretch out a little."

"And I have alterations to do," Mrs. Pye said.

"Oh please!" scoffed Sam. "You mean your chain gang of *butterflies* have alterations to do. They're sweatshop butterflies!" Sam held forth on the victimization of insects all the way back to rehearsal.

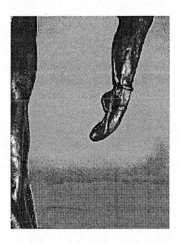

Chapter 3:

In the Men's Dressing Room

The early December air smelled sharply of woodfires burning in home hearths, but the delicious smell of the season and the early bloom of post-Thanksgiving Christmas decorations were lost on Sam.

"I just wasn't ready for it, that's all," she grumped as she kicked a pile of dead leaves.

"What do you mean, you weren't ready for it? Nothing's happened." Katy, who was enjoying being outdoors for a change and wanted to savor this short walk before the long stressful ordeal of dress rehearsal, was beginning to lose patience with Sam's impatience. It was not the first time in the last two months that this had been true, but in spite of the sharp differences in temperament that sometimes caused sparks to fly, Sam had become the closest friend and confidante that Katy had ever had.

"Exactly! Nothing!" Sam whined. "I mean, there was this huge build-up and *you* had all these wild experiences and neat stuff, and then as soon as *I* get involved... Nothing! Zero! Zip! Nada! Just rehearsals, school, rehearsals, ballet classes, rehearsals, homework, rehearsals, and-- oh yes--more rehearsals. In the last two months I've had even fewer supernatural encounters than I've had home-cooked meals."

"Oh, *I'm* sorry," Katy replied with a clearly sarcastic edge on her voice. "We just misunderstood each other. See, I thought the whole reason Mrs. Pye hooked us up was so you could *prevent* exciting things from happening. Things like *death.* You know most people find everyday life interesting enough if it just involves normal, *un*exciting things like working in a huge dance production with professional dancers and choreographers and sitting in on mind-reading lessons while pretending to be a boy. Even if they never get to be chained in the attic of a child-stealing monster. You know you can't have everything."

Sam shot her a baleful look. "Some monster! The only diabolical thing the guy has done has been to fuss over the Blonde Bimbo Ballerina till we're all ready to throw up. I don't know how you can stand being in the same rehearsal with those two."

"Part of the job," Katy shrugged. She didn't particularly enjoy her work as Brianna's understudy, but she did it as professionally as she could. "So are your parents coming tomorrow night?" Katy asked with a masterful change of topic.

"Opening night? Every relative I have is going to be there!" Sam's excitement about her first real performance was clear: her shoulders lifted up around her ears, her wide grin split her face into two happy halves, and if the phrase "stars in her eyes" hadn't already been invented, any passing on-looker would have come up with it. "How about yours?"

"They're waiting for my Clara performance."

"Well, yeah, I guess that makes sense." As a rule Sam tip-toed around the subject of Katy's parents. In her opinion, Katy was an unusually gifted, possibly brilliant dancer, and she thought Rebecca and Michael Moon didn't provide her with nearly enough encouragement and support. But she didn't want to say so since Katy didn't. Sam's own Mother had bought tickets for almost every performance.

"Yeah, I mean, it's not like it's my first *Nut*. But I'd almost rather they came to see me do 'Snow.' "

"No kidding? Why?"

"Well, it's more interesting choreography for one thing. It's all that soft lyrical stuff that really suits my body. Technically it's a lot harder than Clara. I guess I'm prouder of being able to do it. And it's *mine*, you know? It's my real part. Clara is really Brianna's part."

They sat on the steps of the Opera House a few moments, eating granola bars and watching a man on a ladder winding a string of lights into the branches of a tree.

Since she had started doing *Nutcrackers* four years ago, Katy had been too busy every year as Christmas approached to participate much in the universal ramp-up to the holidays. She had the urge to shop and wrap and decorate and ice Christmas cookies like everyone else. There just weren't enough hours left over in her week. She thought to herself with a small sigh that it was true; you really can't have everything.

"I watched 'Snow' last night from the wings," Sam said. "You really *are* good in it."

"Thanks."

"Does Lise Moreau ever say anything?"

Katy thought about the question. "Not very often. I mean everybody rehearses without saying much--"

"The boys don't," Sam scoffed.

"Well, yeah, but they're different. The girls mostly just ask a question now and then. I don't think Lise even does that. But she doesn't really need to. I've never seen her talk to any of the other dancers--not even her partner."

"Creepy."

"Yeah. But I know a lot of girls who would give up talking if it meant they could dance like that."

"Even creepier." Sam had not yet bought into the ballet mind-set that all sacrifices were reasonable if made in the name of Art and Career.

They entered the stage door of the Opera House, and wandered slowly down the hall looking for their dressing room assignments. On each dressing room door was taped a list of the characters who would use that room.

The first room was assigned to Mirlitons, Arabian, Spanish, Chinese, and Russian. The second room was reserved for Mice and Mother Ginger's Children. The third room was labeled only "Men."

For the first time it occurred to Katy that Sam would be expected to dress in the boys' dressing room, and it shocked her into dropping her dance bag.

"Sam!" she said. "You have to dress with the *boys*!"

Sam shrugged. "Big deal. I have brothers."

Katy could only sputter in protest. "But you can't get undressed in there!   And *they'll* all be undressed in there!"

Sam did indeed look a little uncomfortable, but clearly she wasn't going to back out now. "We're still really early," she said.   "Maybe I can get in and out before anybody else arrives."

Katy stood watching in horror as Sam took a deep breath and pushed open the door.   Inside there was only one person, Tanya, sitting with her feet up on a dressing table, her chair leaning back at a perilous angle, reading a magazine.   As Sam entered, she looked up briefly, then looked back down at the article she was reading.

"Evenin', Sam," she said casually.

"Hi, Miss Tanya," Sam said, deepening her voice just a touch.

She started to walk past Tanya to the costume rack, but the rehearsal mistress, without looking up from her reading, swung one leg across the aisle and propped her foot against the wall, blocking Sam's path.

Katy grabbed the door before it swung completely shut, holding it open just enough to watch through the crack.

"Where ya' headed, Sam?"

"Uh.. I was gonna get changed..."

"Not in here... 'Sam.' "

"'Scuse me, ma'am?"

Tanya had still not lifted her eyes from the magazine.   "It is my professional opinion, 'Sam,' that you do not have the basic equipment required to dress in this room."   Now she looked up, sternly.   "Don't believe you could pass the physical."

Sam had turned the color of the red soldiers' jackets hanging at the back of the room. "Busted," she whispered hoarsely.

"Indeed."   Tanya stood up, folded her magazine, and headed out the door, almost knocking over the eavesdropping Katy and calling back over her shoulder, "You'll find your costume hanging in Dressing Room 6. With 'Snow.'" And with a wicked wink at Katy, she was gone down the hall.

Sam crept shamefacedly out of the dressing room into the hallway. She and Katy stared at each other wide-eyed for about three long seconds, then both erupted into hysterical, uncontrollable laughter that left them rolling on the floor, gasping for breath, tears streaming down their faces.

While they were lying there, one of the male soloists walked up, a cup of coffee in his hand. He paused, reluctant to step over them to get in the door of the men's dressing room, and said, "Ummm... could I...?"

Which sent them into another fit of helpless laughter as they half-rolled, half-crawled away from the door.

Chapter 4:

The Search for Albinoni

It took Katy and Sam a good ten minutes to bring themselves to a sitting position, backs against the wall, and wipe the tears off their cheeks.

"How long do you suppose she's known?" Katy asked when she could to talk.

"No idea," gasped Sam. "But she never let on *at all.* I truly thought I had pulled it off. Do you think I should go apologize?"

"At least. But I think you should wait till you have a box of candy or some flowers in your hand before you try it."

Sam got to her feet and extended her hand to help Katy up. "Yeah. And a picture of me with a bow in my hair and a mustache. Come on, Snowflake. Let's go get changed."

The dress rehearsal was agonizingly long and included all the usual disasters of a final run-through with a huge cast and complicated technical problems.

Entrances were missed. Lights didn't work. The wrong music came on at the start of the second act. The huge Christmas tree that "magically" grows from six feet to twenty got stuck half-way up. A soloist threw a pointe shoe at her partner. One of Mother Ginger's Children burst into tears and refused to come out from under her skirts, and another wet her pants.

Katy had her customary ambivalence about dancing in her costume. It was itchy and the sleeves bothered her where they draped down over the tops of her shoulders and hampered her arm movements, but she looked gorgeous in it, and she knew it.

Sam, feeling that she owed Tanya something for having let her get away with gender fraud, danced her heart out and out-jumped every real boy on-stage. Tanya grinned evilly at her from the wings, but Sam couldn't get up the nerve to talk to her yet.

When the curtain call had been set and practiced three times, and the mothers of the youngest cast members were starting to drag them off home without waiting for permission, the rehearsal finally sputtered to a halt.

Everyone was reminded of call times for the performance, and the dancers were dismissed except for an unlucky few that Langford kept to make some detailed corrections with the music.

Sam and Katy dragged themselves back to their dressing room to change and remove their make-up. Brianna was also assigned to their dressing room, and as Katy smeared cleansing cream all over her face, Brianna slid into the chair beside hers. In the make-up mirrors, Katy could see that Brianna was lit up like a Christmas tree, and Katy told her she had danced beautifully.

Brianna beamed. "Thanks," she grinned. "Mr. Langford's been working with me a lot." She leaned on her elbows and stared at her reflection thoughtfully in the mirror. "You know, Katy, because of Mr. Langford, for the first in as long as I can remember, I don't feel like a failure. Like maybe I can dance after all." A small private smile played around the edges of her mouth. "I feel like my life is finally beginning."

Katy tried to return Brianna's happy smile, but it didn't quite reach all the way to her eyes. Katy turned back to her own image in the mirror.

The mirror, however, no longer held her reflection. Instead, it held a handwriting that Katy had come to dread.

ॐ

11 September
Padua, Italy

My heart plummets from hope to despair and rebounds again to hope with each knock at my door. Musician after musician is admitted to the upper chamber where Galina rocks and weeps. Each plays for her. Each is packed off again. Galina rocks and weeps, rocks and weeps...

At each failure, I rage at her and at the nameless old woman. Each time the crone laughs and spins a web of words that bind me up in the hope of possessing Galina, her lithe body and her wild soul together, for eternity.

Though she drinks a little, Galina yet refuses all food. She grows each day weaker, and seems to neither see nor hear me nor to feel my riding crop when it bites into her.

The crone calls me now.   Another band of musicians awaits. I dare not hope again. My heart is too weary.

&

What a joyful difference the last hour has wrought!

The stone walls of the chamber seemed to soften and melt as these musicians played! The melody spoke of tragedy and hope, of acceptance and struggle, of yearning for something lost and reaching toward some possible triumph.

Galina stopped her agonized rocking as the music filled the room around her. Her eyes lifted to watch the cellist's bow move across the strings, and she released her grasp on her bare legs. When the last strain died away, she lay quietly asleep on the floor.

I lifted her and brought her to the bed she has refused to use. I covered her gently, and then ushered the musicians into the hall, where I promised them a year's employment and told them to return tomorrow morning.

It is their leader who wrote this aching melody that soothed Galina into peaceful sleep--Tomaso Albinoni by name. He begged off, pleading his commitments in Venice, but sold me the work, "Adagio in G minor," outright and left his musicians to play it at my pleasure.

At last I, too, shall close my eyes once more in grateful sleep, confident of peaceful dreams and a happier tomorrow.

&

"Katy?" Sam's voice reached her as if from down a long hallway. "Katy? Mission control calling Katy. Come in, Katy."

"Huh? Sorry." Katy shook her head.

"I *said*, can I use your brush?"

"Sure. Here."

"Thanks."   Sam started brushing her thick dark hair out of its neatly parted Soldier arrangement upward into the spikey mess she preferred. "I'm really getting used to this haircut. Think I'll keep it this way."

"Sam?" Katy asked, wiping the cream off her face with a tissue, "do you know anything about a composer named Albinoni?"

ॐ

As soon as she got home that night, Katy headed straight to the game room and sat down at the computer.

A search for "Albinoni" brought up a long list of music sites.   The first one was just an e-commerce site selling classical CD's, and the second was in German, but the third read:

"ALBINONI, Tomaso; Italian composer(1671-1750). Best known during his lifetime for his many operas, Albinoni's comtemporary reputation is based primarily on the 'Adagio in G minor.' The work as we know it, however, is not the original; the 'Adagio' was reconstructed in the 1940's from a fragment of bassline.   The original work vanished during Albinoni's lifetime and has never been recovered."

Katy quickly checked three more sites and found the same basic information: Tomaso Albinoni, prolific composer, native of Venice, born 1671, died 1750.

Hugh Langford had purchased the "Adagio in G minor" from Albinoni himself three hundred years ago.

Chapter 5:

Curtain

"Opening night." Within those two words lie all possibilities: triumph, transcendence, vindication, failure, disgrace, disappointment.

In practice, opening night usually contains all of them in at least infinitesimal amounts.

Backstage, as the call for "Places" went out, Katy and Sam hugged each other tightly and whispered, "Merde," the French curse that serves as a dancer's pre-performance good-luck charm.

Sam would dance before Katy, but first came the Party Scene, which, Sam insisted, was so long and boring that "People grow old and die" before the end.

Finally Brianna/Clara's precious nutcracker was bestowed, broken, and mended, the guests were dispatched, midnight struck, and Christmas tree grew--all twenty feet this time.

Enter the Mice in their much-despised masks. Enter the Soldiers to do battle with them and their leader, the evil Rat King.

The cast was huge: over a hundred, ranging in age from four-year-olds to a beloved octogenarian dance teacher whose part called for him only to totter energetically across the stage waving a cane at a naughty child. Because of the unmanageable number of dancers, the area in the wings was forbidden to any performer not in the current scene or the one immediately following. It was patrolled by a humorless stage manager, and trespassers were evicted without mercy.

Fortunately, 'Snow' followed the Battle Scene, so Katy was able to watch as her best friend stepped on-stage, black eyes flashing with excitement and terror.

As usual, there was some degradation of technique--feet slightly less pointed, legs not quite at their maximum in the grands battements, a slight catch-step when the adrenaline rush pushed her just a fraction off the music. But there was a compensating electricity in her movements that told Katy that, technical flaws notwithstanding, the girl could *dance*.

All the rest was details that could be easily ironed out with just ten or twelve years of relentless, single-minded effort.

Katy's heart swelled with affection and pride for her friend, her best friend, the person (next to her father) that she loved best in the world.

Sam came offstage and fell into Katy's waiting arms. "I was *awful!*" came the whispered broken-hearted wail.

"No you weren't! You were great!"

"I almost fell on the first jump!"

"Nobody could tell. I didn't see it, and I was watching."

"Really? Are you sure?"

"I swear." The other Snowflakes had already formed their lines, prancing their feet up and down, taking deep second-position pliés to stretch hamstrings, shaking out their hands to relax their fingers. "Gotta go."

"Merde, Katy!"

A quick hug, and white clouds of Snowflakes drifted off, turning lazily. Katy took her place with the other three Attendants and, carried on the crest of the musical swell, preceded the Snow Queen in the stage-run that had finally been mastered to Tanya's satisfaction.

The waltz took six minutes. For six minutes Katy hovered in the strange on-stage state of performers where awareness is heightened to such a razor's edge that all events outside the hotly illuminated rectangle of stage, all moments outside the fierce intensity of Now and Here, lose their reality and become dimly irrelevant.

It is a process wherein a private spiritual state is attained through a public physical act. If barre was Katy's refuge from the world, during her moments on-stage she stepped out to the face the world, looked above it, and spoke with God. For six minutes.

The heavy velvet curtain drew slowly closed across the still-circling dancers, separating them once more from the unseen audience, returning them and their applauding watchers to their separate realities.

She remembered every minuscule detail of position and movement from the six minutes, but the ecstasy, the exultation, was, as always, lost until the next time she stood in the wings, blood roaring as loudly as the music, waiting to fling herself back into the infinite.

Katy knew she had danced well. Not perfectly--never perfectly--but well, and a residual radiance hung about her, which she savored. She left the stage slowly, wanting to postpone its loss as long as possible.

The rest of the evening was a happy jumble of playing cards with Sam in the dressing room while waiting out the second act, then the chaotic scramble through the curtain call, followed almost immediately by the backstage invasion of friends and relatives who clogged every square foot of the hallways to congratulate the dancers.

Katy was hugged and kissed by Sam's mother until her bun collapsed. Katy adored short, round, enthusiastic Mrs. Mia, from whom Sam had inherited her exotic eyes and black hair, and she happily allowed herself to be passed around and introduced to a dozen short, dark-eyed relatives.

A few moments later, Sam's father came working his way through the sea of family members, pushing Sam's six-year-old brother Zachery ahead of him and toward Katy. Zachery was looking back at his father, his big brown eyes pleading to be excused, but he was propelled inexorably forward.

When they stood directly in front of Katy, Mr. Mia gave a final shove, and Zachery, eyes glued to the floor, extended his small fist which throttled one slightly mangled tulip, its lower stem carefully wrapped in damp paper towel and aluminum foil.

"This is for you," he croaked.

"Why, Zachery!" Katy exclaimed. "It's beautiful! Thank you!" She bent down and hugged the little boy who grinned even as he squirmed away from the embrace.

"He picked it himself," Mr. Mia announced. "But next time, he's going to ask first before he pulls flowers out of the neighbor's flowerbed, aren't you, son?"

Zachery ducked his head and beat a strategic retreat from his father's stern warning look.

Above the noisy throng of backstage well-wishers, Jennifer Sandropol's head appeared as she called to ask if Katy needed a ride.

"No, she's coming with us," called back Mrs. Mia. "You'll come to our house, Katy. We'll have a late supper, and you'll spend the night. I already told your mother."

"She started cooking around Halloween," Sam whispered. "Sort of a Tex-Mex-Amerindian-Greco-Italian smorgasbord." The Mias' ethnic origins were shrouded in mystery and confusion, and they freely adopted any cultural affiliations that struck their fancy.

"No Inuit?" Katy asked.

"For dessert. But don't ask for a big piece if you're not crazy about walrus."

Sam began to edge toward the stage door, and the Mia clan moved as though attached to her, much as bees clustered around their queen can be moved in a buzzing clump.

Katy and Sam led the hive of Mias toward the parking lot. To Katy's left was the open doorway of the performer's lounge, traditionally known as the Green Room.

Katy's passing glance was caught by the sight of Hugh Langford, sitting on the Green Room couch next to Brianna, placing a small bouquet of pale sweetheart roses in her hands. Langford placed a finger under Brianna's chin, lifting it to look into his face as he spoke softly to her. Brianna was smiling and crying.

It was an intensely private moment, and Katy averted her eyes, looking quickly to the right.

Directly beside Katy stood Lise Moreau, who saw the pair a split second after Katy did, and jerked backwards, as if slapped in the face. The beautiful ballerina, so flawless in every physical detail, having just performed her solo with exquisite precision, backed away down the hall as if in fear, her green eyes filled with jealous tears. Katy would have sworn that she bared her teeth and *hissed*.

The crowd surged between them, Lise was gone, and Katy was caught up again by the festive Mias and carried off to an opening night celebration that rolled merrily on long after Katy and Sam had collapsed in exhaustion on Sam's bed, asleep before they could even get their clothes off.

Chapter 6:

Moon Matinee

The Nutcracker ran for three weeks, five performances a week, including the Saturday matinees, fifteen performances in all.

The first week of the run, a nasty flu epidemic cut a swath through the cast, leaving miserable, feverish dancers in its wake. Katy missed several days of school and then had to do a lot of fast talking to get permission to perform anyway.

Sam assumed an air of metabolic superiority and lectured all and sundry about anti-oxidants and the immune system until the wheezing, hacking cast members threatened to evict her from the dressing room if she didn't shut up.

Twenty-four hours later Sam was as sick as the rest, and accused the Snowflakes of deliberately sneezing on her.

Between school, homework, and performances Katy managed to squeeze in one trip to the mall to buy Christmas presents. For Sam she got a pair of woolly warm-up pants made like knitted overalls and a miniature toy soldier.

She bought perfume for her mother (who always exchanged her gifts the day after Christmas, so why kill yourself picking something?), a blown glass paperweight for her father, who had been known to get lost for half an hour staring at some beautiful, useless things, and two of her favorite Christmas books for the twins: *The Littlest Angel* and *The Snow Queen*, both with fabulous illustrations.

She had the hardest time finding something for Mrs. Pye until she saw a wild pair of striped knee socks made so that each toe had its own separate compartment like the fingers in a glove, each toe in a different brightly colored yarn.

She laughed out loud as she paid for them, imagining them peeking out from under the silk patches and layers of shawls.

Katy's performance as Clara fell on the last Saturday of the run, and her mother packed the house with every friend and relative that she could bully into buying a ticket. Backstage after the performance, Katy was inundated with bouquets of flowers, all seeming to contain the identical six carnations, three daisies, two sprigs of baby's breath, and one stick of some crispy-dry purple thing.

"Do you think they all went together to buy them?" Sam wondered, staring at the bundles lined up like little soldiers on a table in the dressing room, each with a sheet of pink cellophane stapled around it.

Katy snorted. "Are you kidding? My mother ordered them wholesale and passed them out like you do confetti at a New Year's Eve party."

"Well," said Sam doubtfully, "I guess it's still a nice gesture."

"All part of her Mother-of-the-Star role. If I hadn't stopped her, she'd have made them all troop up to the stage during my bow and lay them at my feet adoringly. Guess we'd better get out there. My public awaits."

The assemblage of Moon-affiliates was indeed impressive. They milled around the lobby like penned cattle, anxious to be let out of the corral. Rebecca Moon held them there by sheer force of will, waiting for Katy to make an appearance. When she did, they burst into applause. Katy, trying to be a good sport despite her embarrassment, curtseyed to the crowd.

She did a masterful job of dealing with her mother's guests. She visited with them two by two just long enough to provide them with an opening to glance at their watch and comment on the lateness of the hour and how they had told the baby-sitter, etc. Two by two she bestowed parting kisses, feeling them sigh with relief as they waved themselves out the door to their cars.

"Boy, are you good!" observed Sam appreciatively. "Can you teach me how to do that, or is it something only a Delven Maiden can do?"

"Skill born of desperation," Katy replied as she moved on to dispose of the last pair of ancient aunts. They were allowed to coo over her for fifteen seconds before Katy's remark about the sky looking like snow sent them scurrying off to pilot their enormous vintage Buick home "before it hits."

As Katy turned around, she was surprised to see Hugh Langford deep in conversation with her mother, who held one of Katy's bouquets to her face, smelling it coquettishly.

Katy watched them carefully, trying to assess whether or not she should go join the conversation. It was more prudent for her to stay at arm's length from Mr. Langford. Plus, Rebecca Moon looked like a woman who would not appreciate having her discussion with this gorgeous director cut short by her teen-aged daughter.

The problem was that her mother was fully capable of standing there fluttering her eyelashes at the man until time for the evening performance, and Katy was tired.

She started to move toward them, pulling Sam along with her, but the two girls were intercepted by Katy's father.

"Hey, Elf. Can a mere dad get an autograph from the star?"

Katy gave a mock sigh. "I suppose so. But only one. My agent is *very* strict about that." She threw her arms around his neck, letting him pick her up by the waist and swing her around once.

When he set her down he turned to Sam and shook her hand solemnly. "Fine performance, my lad," he said formally.

"Thank you, sir," replied Sam in the deepest baritone she could manage. Sam's boy impersonation had amused Michael Moon hugely, and the two of them had constructed an elaborate man-to-man routine around it.

"Are you two coming home or staying here between your shows?"

"Staying here," said Katy. "But I could use a burger. As soon as Mom's ready to go." Rebecca showed no signs of releasing Hugh Langford from her conversational clutches.

Michael looked over at his wife and the director. Katy thought she saw her father shiver in distaste. "That guy with the patch..." he said.

"Mr. Langford?"

"Yeah. Is it just me, or is he..."

"Creeped out?" offered Sam.

"Not the precise phrasing I was looking for, but close to the spirit of it," laughed Michael. "Something about him seems off-center or something."

"Not just you," Katy assured him. "He is *way* off-center. Hey, Daddy? Are you coming to any other performances?"

"Well, small elf daughter, your mother hadn't planned anything. Did you want me to? There's just tonight and tomorrow, right?"

Katy felt the hesitancy she always felt when asking for her father's attention. As though, on a very deep level, she was afraid that any imposition might shatter the relationship. "You don't have to," she assured him quickly. "It's not a big deal."

"Are you going to be Carol again?"

"Clara, Daddy."

Michael grinned. He knew perfectly well the name of the character.

"No, this was my only performance as Clara, but..."

"But the other part she dances is really more important, even if it's not a solo," put in Sam, seeing that Katy wasn't going to cut to the chase. "It's more difficult choreography, and for her as a dancer, it's more... more..."

"Professionally significant?" Michael asked. Both girls nodded. "Then I should come and see it, shouldn't I?" He smiled warmly at his daughter.

Katy returned the smile shyly. "But you don't *have* to. You came once."

"I'm really buried in work this weekend, but I'll see what I can do," he promised. Katy felt hope build temptingly in her, but she didn't want to give it much room to take hold. Her father wasn't the best at carving out whole evenings to sit through dance performances.

She knew he loved her. Even better, she knew he understood her. Unfortunately, she never aroused the same sense of urgency in him that a business crisis did. And there was always a business crisis. She understood; but it saddened her. She felt that something precious between them was slipping away, like sand dropping through fingers that weren't held tightly enough, and he didn't feel it happening.

Sam, seeing that an opportunity was about to be lost for lack of specificity, said, "Here's what you should do: 'Snow' is the very last thing in the first act. Come about thirty minutes late, stand in the back, and then you can leave at intermission, okay?"

Katy's father pursed his lips, reviewing in his mind the contents of his brief case.

"*Okay?*" Sam insisted.

"I'll try, girls. That's the most I can say right now."

Katy knew what that meant. She hugged him anyway, partly to hide her disappointment, partly because she needed the physical contact with him, her beloved workaholic father with eyebrows like her own. "I'm starved, Daddy," she said as she inhaled the nice daddy-smell of his jacket. "Let's go eat, okay?"

After their burgers, Sam, who was still recovering from her flu, found an unoccupied corner of a couch in the green room and took a nap. Katy got a diet Coke out of the machine and, sitting on the floor beside Sam, started thumbing idly through one of the programs, reading the ads that all seemed to say the same thing: "Best

Wishes to City Dance Council from the Acme Insurance Agency."

"Sam!" she whispered, whacking the sleeping Soldier on the hip. Sam grumbled but didn't open her eyes. Katy whacked again. "Look! Can you read this?"

Sam opened one eye part way. "Best Wishes to..."

"No! *This* page!"

Sam opened both eyes. She sat up. Over Katy's shoulder she read

17 September
Padua, Italy
Each day the musicians play the Adagio for Galina. Each day she rides the swell of their music closer to life and to me.

She eats a little--delicate dishes which I feed her from my hand. I dress her each morning in velvet and pearls. When she cries, I beat her and send away her musicians. When she stops, I bring them back and brush her hair with a silver comb while she listens.

Three days ago she stood and swayed gently while they played. The next, the old woman came and whispered in her ear as the music started, and she danced a few tentative steps as I stared greedily.

The old woman drew me aside. "Now you must decide," she told me. "She will dance for you now. You can train her as you train your dogs and horses. She is coming to believe that she cannot survive without your approval. You mean music and dance to her; and for her, music and dance are life. Are you content with that? Is it enough?"

I considered this as I watched Galina moving slowly to the music. She is exquisite. I own her almost as completely as I own my sculptures. But when I look into her eyes, there is a spark, a tiny flame of self that still burns independently of me, that belongs only to her. This last scrap of self, this tiny un-possessed corner of her soul taunts, infuriates me.

"No," I told the crone. "It is not enough."

She smiled and rubbed her hands together. "Then we have work to do!" she crowed, grinning as she slowly pulled my dagger from its sheath at my belt. "Blood work."

I drew back in sudden apprehension. I knew not what she meant to do and demanded her intentions.

"Cut you a window into your soul," she whispered, "for the girl to crawl in."

I pushed the old woman to the ground and wrested my dagger from her hand. She merely shrugged and said, "There's no gift given without a price, my lord. The greater the gift, the more costly."

Without a word I turned back to Galina. She ceased her dancing as I approached her. She looked up at me, and I motioned her to begin again. Obediently enough, she turned from me and retook her starting position.

But not before I glimpsed in her eye a flash of quick resentment, a moment of self-belonging that named me an intruder in her life. That named herself the rightful mistress of that life and dismissed me. With that momentary look she doomed herself. And me, perhaps.

I jerked the old woman upright, my face inches from her own, and held out my knife to her. "Do it!"

I spat out. "But if you fail, old woman, I promise you that you will spend the rest of your life in greater agony than I!"

She sits before my fire now, heating the knife blade in the coals. She will not tell me more of what she plans, and I greatly fear her ungentle hand. But Galina I will have, body and soul, mind and will, no matter the cost.

And if, as the crone promises, it gets me long life in the bargain, so much the better.

Chapter 7

I Am Twelve

Katy was tense and jumpy backstage before the curtain, badly rattled by the journal entry. The lives she read about in the ghostly pages were now too real to her. The slow unfolding of Hugh Langford's grotesque metamorphosis, the tragic fate of the child Galina, seemed to be pressing into her own life with an ominous weight. It was like a nightmare in which she was watching a terrible accident happen in slow motion, wanting to stop it or at least call out a warning, but unable to make a sound or a movement.

During the performance, as the Snowflakes gathered in the wings, she sneaked stage-right to peek between the curtain and the side of the proscenium arch, hoping to catch sight of her father. By the time the stage manager caught her and sent her to places, she still hadn't seen him, and during her dance, the lights shone in her eyes too brightly to see to the back of the auditorium.

Her assumption was that he hadn't come. She hadn't really expected him to.

She was short-tempered even with Sam during the second act, and after the curtain call, she went back to the dressing room, took off her shoes and slammed them into her dance bag. As she prepared to get out of her long white "Snow" costume, Brianna rushed up to her and took both of Katy's hands in her own.

"Oh, Katy, I'm not supposed to tell, but I can't stand it a minute longer!"

"What? Tell me!"

"Well, you know Mr. Langford has been so wonderful to me, and he's helped me so much with my dancing?"

Katy felt her heart start to chill. She knew what was coming. And she knew that she must try to stop it. She just had no idea how.

"You're dancing really well, Brianna. But it's not Mr. Langford. It's you. With any good teacher..."

"That's not true, Katy. I never realized it before, but like he explained to me, some dancers have to have one special teacher who believes in them, who devotes himself to that one student, or she never learns to dance to her full potential."

The girl's eyes were shining with tears of happiness now, and Katy reached out to touch her arm, wanting to warn her, wanting to stop her next words before they could be said out loud.

"And Katy?" Brianna continued, her hands clasped tightly in front of her as the tears now spilled over and ran down her cheeks, "he says he wants to be that teacher for me! I'm going to be his private student! And live in his house and train with him every single day! I won't even go to regular school, I'll have a tutor, and..."

Behind her Katy heard something fall heavily to the ground. A girl gave a little shriek, followed by the gasps of several others.

She turned and saw Lise Moreau in a crumpled heap of white tulle on the floor, her Snow Queen tiara lying beside her.

Katy was vaguely aware of the dressing room door opening and people running down the hall. Other girls were patting Lise's hands and cheeks, calling her name.

Katy spun around toward Sam, who was instantly by her side. "I need to get close to her," Katy whispered. "But I don't think I can get past all those older girls."

Sam dashed to the sink, jerked a handful of paper towels out of the holder, and wet them thoroughly. She grabbed Katy's hand and said loudly and authoritatively, "Here, I have water. Excuse me. Pardon me, could I get through? I have some water."

The crowd of white tutus parted magically. Sam thrust the wet towels into Katy's hand and pushed her toward the fallen ballerina.

Katy knelt beside Lise and carefully applied the towels to her forehead, softly calling her name.

"Everybody move back, she needs air," Sam directed. Impelled by the decisiveness of the tiny girl's voice, they did, leaving only Katy next to her.

"Lise? Lise... Can you hear me?" Katy lowered her head so that she was whispering into Lise's ear, "Please, Lise. If you can hear me, open your eyes. I need your help. Brianna needs your help."

Lise's eyelids flew open. She started to breath in sharp, jerky gasps, staring frantically around herself until her eyes locked with Katy's. She reached up and grabbed the front of Katy's costume, ripping the satin so that the little pearl beads fell in a soft patter to the floor.

"No!" She gasped. "No! No!"

Katy leaned even closer to her. "No, what, Lise?"

"Tell her! Don't go! Stop him!" She was breathing so rapidly that Katy was afraid she would hyperventilate and faint again.

"It's all right, Lise," Katy said soothingly, "I'll tell her. Can you help me tell her? Can you explain to her?"

Lise's only reply was to shake her head wildly from side to side, panic stricken.

"Okay. It's okay," Katy soothed. She thought for a moment. "Lise? Lise listen to me..." Lise focused with difficulty on Katy's face. "Lise, can you help me? Can you help me stop him? Can you tell me how?"

Doubt and fear clouded Lise's eyes. She started to shake her head "no" again but with a mighty effort, stopped and nodded "yes" just once.

"Good," said Katy, "you'll help me, okay? You'll tell me how, and I'll stop him. How do I stop him, Lise?"

Lise was weeping and coughing now, tears running freely down her face, her mouth contorting with her effort to speak.

"Help me, Lise," Katy insisted. "Help Brianna. Tell me how to stop him. If you can't say it, just *think* it, Lise. I can hear it if you think it."

Katy let her mind fall into Lise's. It was like falling into a dark pit. In the pit boiled a blackness and a despair horrible beyond death. Katy recoiled and almost withdrew, but then deliberately released her hold on the brightly lit dressing room, like letting go of a rope, and dropped into the horror, listening and calling Lise's name as she fell.

"Twelve..." she heard Lise's shattered mind say. *"I am Twelve. Now there are enough of us. I know. They told me..."*

Her thought broke off like a scream, but in a moment Katy could make out, *"He keeps our shoes. If you call them, they will come...."*

Hurried footsteps were nearing the dressing room. Lise grabbed her more tightly, staring into her eyes. *"By the water elms..."* her thoughts came faintly. Lise was slipping down further into the darkness and would soon be out of reach even of Katy's mind.

"Put the shoes by the water elms and call us... All of us... The Twelve..."

Then Katy felt only blackness.

Chapter 8:

I Know a Game Worth Two of That

The door to the dressing room flew open, and Tanya strode in, calm and confident, already directing people as she elevated Lise's feet.

A man with a cell phone stuck his head in and said that he had called 911 and the paramedics would be here in a moment.

Tanya nodded and observed that Lise probably just hadn't eaten today and she'd be fine. She gave the dancers instructions, little errands to do to take their minds off the unconscious ballerina. Told them to hang up their costumes. Told them where to go meet their mothers. Reminded them that they had left their school books or their purses on the shelves. Gradually the room cleared.

In the confusion, Sam managed to throw a coat over Katy's costume. She maneuvered her friend out of the dressing room and down the hallway to a secluded corner.

She needed a few minutes. Katy would move when told to, but she didn't speak, her eyes were dilated, and there was no sign of awareness in them. Sam could hardly just go dump Katy in her mother's car in that condition.

Sam sat with her, touching her hands and trying to call her back from the place where her mind was caught. Katy wasn't responding, at least not very quickly, and Sam was looking around as she called, trying to spot Mrs. Pye.

Sam had watched in fury as Hugh Langford came to the door of the dressing room and collected Brianna, comforting her and never even glancing down at Lise where she lay on the floor.

She had watched the paramedics come and put Lise on stretcher and take her off to the emergency room, Tanya striding alongside to handle details as always.

Sam was really worried about Katy now, and she was trying to decide whether or not she should go to look for help--maybe even stop the ambulance before it left the parking lot. Then as she looked into Katy's eyes and called her name once more, Katy's pupils began to contract back to their normal size, and Sam saw her friend rise to the surface like a swimmer after a deep dive.

"Sam," Katy whispered weakly, "we have to find Mrs. Pye. I know how she can stop Hugh Langford. Lise told me...."

"Okay, sure," said Sam. "We'll tell her. But tomorrow, okay? Right now we need to get you home. Tomorrow we'll come early and... "

Around a corner of the long hallway came Hugh Langford. Brianna was at his side, and they were absorbed in each other, deep in fascinated conversation.

"Come on, Katy," Sam insisted. "We're outta here. Now!"

She grabbed Katy's hand and jerked her toward the series of three big double metal doors,

one behind the other that led from the backstage
to the outside.   Katy followed wearily, too
exhausted to protest.

As they reached the exit, Katy glanced toward
Brianna where she stood looking up adoringly at
Hugh Langford. He was bent over her, laughing
in agreement at something she had said.

Katy reflected momentarily that if she hadn't
known better, she would have thought they were
father and daughter, they were both so beautiful,
and seemed so... close. She almost wished...

Hugh Langford's attention was pulled from
Brianna to something far down the hallway.

His smile changed just slightly--just the
tiniest alterations in the facial muscles that made
the difference between a smile of engaging charm
and one of archly malicious triumph.

Katy followed his glance to the other end of
the hallway.

Mrs. Pye was walking steadily toward
Langford, silk patches flowing around her. But as
she came, it seemed to Katy that her skirts were
transforming into something even more fluid, less
solid than silk.

Although she was still far down the hallway,
Katy felt a soft breeze start to rise from Mrs. Pye's
movement as she came. It was warm. Very
warm.

At the opposite end, Hugh Langford
straightened himself, still wearing his triumphant
half-smile.

"Katy?" Sam whispered, "I'm just a dumb
Rumin kid, but I don't like the feel of this. Not
even a little bit. Something tells me we need to
get through those doors *now*."

"Do you hear that?" Katy whispered back,
refusing to be pulled.

Sam shook her head. "I don't hear anything except my heart beating a lot louder than it should. Come *on*, Katy!" She tugged Katy's arm, but Katy pulled away from her.

"Listen," Katy breathed. "It's not *your* heart you hear. It's *his*."

She was right. From Hugh Langford's end of the hallway came a deep, low regular double pulse. A heartbeat. A bass sound that was so deep it was hardly audible. But it was palpable through the floor, through the air, through their own bodies as it pushed at the atmosphere around them. It was accompanied by a soft sighing sound. Like breath.

If I were inside a sleeping dragon, Katy thought, this is what it would sound like.

"Good evening, Pye," Hugh Langford called down the hall. "You've met Brianna Wells, I believe?"

His hand fell possessively onto Brianna's shoulder, but Brianna's eyes had gone strangely blank, as though she no longer occupied her body.

"Brianna is my new apprentice. We've just concluded the arrangements with her parents. I think congratulations are in order, don't you?" He laughed hugely, throwing his head back, "Perhaps," he said, opening his free hand in a welcoming gesture, "you'd like to join us in a glass of champagne." He laughed again.

There was no reply. The warm breeze that Katy felt coming from Mrs. Pye increased. It was strong enough now to ruffle Brianna's blond curls, and warm enough so that Katy felt herself start to perspire a little. Carried on the wind was the piercing smell of hot nutmeg.

She could see now what the silk patches were becoming. They were turning into flames.

Now a sound came from Mrs. Pye's end of the hallway, too. Deep rumbling harmonics like a Gregorian chant made by the earth itself. As if the sea and mountains and the sky sang.

As Katy watched, layers of fiery skirts rose behind the old woman, forming enormous wings of flame that reached to the 15-foot ceiling of the hallway. Now her white braids unwound into tongues of flame, running liquid and hot into the air.

Although she was still walking steadily toward Langford, now she seemed not to touch the ground but to float an inch or two above it. The hot wind coming off her made a roaring sound.

Katy glanced at Sam. Sam's eyes had gone as blank as Brianna's and didn't register the transformation of Mrs. Pye into a flaming angel.

Pye had stopped now. She stood--or hovered--about twenty feet from Langford. Katy and Sam were halfway between the two of them. Pye was entirely flame now, her facial features visible only as darker blue-green areas in the brilliant white-yellow-orange fire. The sounds in the hallway were so loud that they hurt Katy's ears. The hot wind whipped Katy's clothing around her.

Pye extended an arm, and a path of fire ran from her flame-fingers across the floor like an arrow shot from a bow, separating Brianna from Langford.

Her earth-harmonics growled deeply, sounding like a "nooooo," rumbled by colliding continental plates.

Hugh Langford took a startled step back from the wall of fire that now separated him from his conquest.

He seemed to consider for a moment, then reached slowly and deliberately to his face with both hands, grasped the patch that covered his right eye, and with a slow smile pulled it down, snapping the cord that held it in place.

"I know a game worth two of that, old woman."

Katy stared in disbelief at the man's face.

Behind the patch was not a blind eye or even a terrible scar. Behind the patch was nothing. An opening into emptiness, like the mouth of a cave, like a window into deep space.

The breath sound increased.

Then, from the emptiness behind his face, came *something.* A vapor. A cold, thick fog that drooled down his face toward the floor like a grotesque tear. It came and came. More and thicker. It fell like a slow-motion waterfall, gathering shape and weight, spreading across the floor. Where it touched Pye's fire, a hissing arose, and the two elements seemed to press against each other, neither able to extinguish the other.

The heart-beat pulse became stronger, more labored, as if under greater and greater effort. Katy saw, pushing out of the empty socket, something gelatinous, something more thickly congealed in the vapor. It fell with a soft "plop" into the bed of fog, heaving and pulsating. Then came another. Then another.

Katy counted them as they were born out of that terrible empty cave. There were twelve.

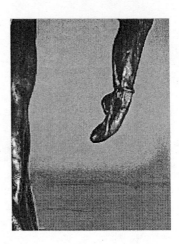

Chapter 9:

Fire and Fog

The twelve *things* seemed to rest a moment, pulsing nauseatingly under the fog. Slowly they began to writhe, shaping themselves by their movements.

Katy watched in horrified fascination as the formless, disgusting lumps gradually became the shapes of children--young girls with flowing hair who moved with the grace of dancers.

Even half-hidden in the dense fog, Katy could see that one of them wore the face of a ten-year-old Lise Moreau.

From where she stood, Katy could only intermittently glimpse Brianna as the waves of flame and fog rose and fell between them. The girl seemed to have gone into a trance; her eyes were open but unseeing.

Katy looked beside her at Sam. She was in the same hypnotized, expressionless state. Katy was the only witness to this battle.

Mrs. Pye's warning came back to her like an echo: *"What has saved you so far, Katy Moon, is that Hugh Langford does not yet know what you are... This is a secret that you must keep from him for as long as you can."*

She made her eyes go blank, relaxing her jaw. If Sam and Brianna were hypnotized, she had to appear to be, too.

The child-shapes now moved in time with the rhythmic sounds that came from Langford, their thin vapor-bodies swaying with his breath, pulsing gently with his heart-beat.

They danced in lovely patterns, sometimes in unison, sometimes in canon, repeating a movement one after the other like waves on a beach. They circled Langford, reaching toward him adoringly. He in turn reached toward them, smiling and lifting their smoke-like hair in his fingers.

At a signal from him they took hands and formed a gracefully moving daisy-chain line, each shape ducking in turn under the arm of another, weaving themselves hypnotically toward Pye's flame wall. As they reached it, the edge where the fog met the flame sizzled angrily. Clouds of black smoke billowed up from the contact. The line of shapes stepped confidently into the flames toward Brianna.

Pye increased her harmonics, pouring more energy out of her body and into her wall. The line of dancing shapes drew back, faltering in their rhythm. Two of them looked back at Langford in confusion.

He motioned them forward again. Again they wound in their delicate patterns around each other, then moved into the fire.

Once more Pye's fire rose higher, impenetrably barring their way.

They drifted back toward Langford, who struck at them impatiently, sweeping his arm through their insubstantial shapes, disrupting their form, scattering them momentarily. As they re-assembled themselves, they seemed to Katy to be weeping silently.

"Ah, Pye," Hugh Langford said sadly when he recovered himself, "you were always the greedy one. Be reasonable, Madame. There is plenty here for us both."

He nodded toward Katy and Sam. "I conceded you this one, didn't I? Now you begrudge me even this other poor scrap of a girl."

He looked genuinely grieved, as though the flaming figure before him had hurt him deeply with her actions.

Pye made no reply. Neither the wall of flame nor its accompanying wild-fire winds diminished.

Katy felt that she was in the center of a fiery hurricane. She kept her face blank, but felt herself begin to lean toward Hugh Langford's cold fog for relief.

"You're working hard, Pye," the man continued. "I wonder how long you can continue this--how much you've left in reserve. Hard to tell," he mused reflectively. "But my guess would be that whatever you have left, it is not enough to fight me on two fronts."

He looked speculatively toward Katy then back at the flaming figure.

"I must have one, Pye. I know you would prefer that I seal myself away in my rooms and starve in slow, solitary splendor. Regretfully, I decline.   But as a gentleman, I offer you your choice."

He gestured elegantly with both hands reaching toward both Katy and Brianna. Still the flaming wall did not move.

With a soft movement, he summoned his vapor shapes and sent them wrapped in their cold fog carpet toward Katy, dipping and gliding in graceful menace.

From Pye's other hand, a second wall of flame shot between Katy and Langford.   It seemed, however, to siphon off some energy from the first wall. Both barriers were lower, gentle tendrils of fire rather than the furnace that had first formed. The sound of her harmonics lightened perceptibly.

In the sighing of his breath, Hugh Langford's sadness called to Katy.   His pain and his loneliness were so like her own.   They belonged together. Her face began to relax its trance-like blankness.

The child-shapes had reached Pye's second wall now. They produced the same hard crackle and sizzle, the same clouds of black smoke.

But the fog-shapes seemed to be slowly, steadily extinguishing the flames. Inch by inch the dancers moved forward through the fire toward Katy.

Hugh Langford lifted one sardonic eyebrow. "Yes," he said softly. "I thought not. You can't do it, Pye.   Not both.   In fact, I doubt you have enough left to protect *yourself* much longer."

He began to chuckle unpleasantly. "If I'm not mistaken, Pye--and I rarely am--you have just enough left to escape. Alone. You can let me have them both now. Or in another few seconds, those flames will go out, and I will have them both anyway, and your death in the bargain.

"For such an eagerly awaited event, I am more than happy to delay my departure a moment or two. Unlike you, my children are not at all tired."

This was true. The lovely dancers were making slow but steady progress through the smoke. They were reaching for Katy, calling her. They were cool and beautiful. They would save her from the terrible fires around her. She felt herself reaching back for them.

Almost before Katy perceived this to be happening, there was a sound like a huge gas jet being lit. The fire of Pye's first wall went out abruptly, and the flames were sucked back into her flaming body and then shot out again to join those protecting Katy.

The vapor-shapes were thrown back violently. Katy could hear their silent cries in her mind.

Through the flames around her, Katy saw Hugh Langford take a step forward in alarm, then smile broadly.

She looked toward Pye, now once again in the form of an old woman, crumpled on the floor, glaring toward Langford. The only part of her that still burned were her eyes. Her harmonics had faded to a weak hum, drowned out by the heart-beat and breath sounds that came more strongly than ever from him. But with one out-stretched hand, she kept the firewall roaring around Katy.

"Interesting," said Hugh Langford. He looked toward Katy, his one eye narrowed in speculation. "What is she to you, old woman? Something so precious that you would sacrifice yourself *and* the other one to keep her from me?" He looked back at Pye. "In a moment that flame, too, will go out. Forever. And then, slowly and deliciously, I shall find out."

The strange tableau stayed frozen for what seemed to Katy like an hour: Hugh Langford, surrounded by his lovely, half-transparent creatures; Brianna, to one side like a beautiful blond doll; Katy and Sam behind a barrier wall of fire that already seemed to grow weaker; the dying Pye on the floor, forcing her last strength into the protective flames.

Katy looked away from the pitiful shape on the floor, and reached eagerly toward Hugh Langford and his twelve children.

The earth-harmonics went abruptly silent, leaving Katy's ears ringing. She did not look again toward Pye.

As she prepared to step happily across the last low flickers of Pye's firewall and claim her place beside Langford, the double metal doors behind her flew open with a "Bang!" that rattled the building. Katy and Sam were blown backwards through the doorway as though from the blast of an explosion, and as they hit the ground, Katy felt the spell woven by Hugh Langford shatter and become terror. Beside her, Sam shook her head, returning to consciousness.

Hugh Langford hurled himself after them, but as he reached the doorway, he was picked up as if by an invisible hand, and thrown back into the hallway away from them. His body was slammed against the far wall, and he screamed in rage and pain.

The next set of doors behind Katy and Sam were also blown open and almost off their hinges, then the third and last pair. Sam grabbed Katy's hand and started dragging her toward the dark outside the building. Katy half-scrambled after her. As they reached the asphalt, they looked back into the corridor behind them.

Hugh Langford had crawled, bleeding and raging, back to the first open doorway but could

not get through it. Something invisible blocked
his way.

Katy, but not Sam, saw twelve vapor-shapes
congealed back into formless lumps that heaved
themselves toward the gaping hole that should
have been an eye socket. One was already oozing
back up into the emptiness behind his face, and
the others were following, quivering in pain and
panic.

Behind him lay Mrs. Pye, lifeless, one hand
still held out toward Katy. The lenses of her little
round glasses were cracked, the wire frames
twisted and tangled crookedly in her disorderly
white hair.

The three pairs of heavy metal doors slammed
shut one at a time, between the girls and the
horror behind them. The sound of their closing
echoed for a long moment in the night.

Chapter 10:

Alone

"Hi, it's me," came Sam's voice over the phone. "Are you okay?"

"Yeah, I'm okay.   Really   tired.   I   had nightmares all night. And sometimes I just start crying."

"I know. Me, too."

"Mrs. Pye..."

"I know. Me, too."

There was a long silence between the two friends.

"So, Katy...? Are you doing the performance tonight?"

"I think I have to. If I didn't, I'd have to give Mom some kind of explanation. And what would I say?"

"I guess you could say you were sick."

"Sam, I haven't even stayed home sick from a ballet *class* in five years. To convince Mom I'm too sick to do a performance I'd have to actually throw up in her lap. Although the way I feel I could probably pull that off."

"So... what do we do? Just kind of get there at the last minute, and stay close together, and leave in a hurry?."

"I guess we could do that. But, Sam?" Doubt and duty battled in Katy's voice. Sam could hear it. "Is that what we *should* do? I keep feeling like there's something more that's expected of me."

"Yeah. I know. Like we've been left in charge. I gotta tell you, Katy, I'm not thrilled with the idea."

"No. Me either. It all seems a lot bigger than me."

"Than both of us."

"But there's nobody else left, is there?"

"Not unless Mrs. Pye left you the Delve web site address and we could email for help."

"No. Nothing. She always said... that when I was ready... she would..." It took her a moment to stop the quiver in her voice.

Sam knew what last night had done to Katy. She was grappling with more than the horrors she had witnessed, or even the loss of a friend she loved; she was facing the loss of her only link to other people like herself.

Sam waited a long moment until she could tell that Katy was back in control of her grief before she said, "So I guess we need a plan, don't we?"

"Actually," Katy said wearily, "I think I've got one. Or at least the beginning of one. You're not going to like it." Katy took a deep breath and outlined her idea.

When she hung up the phone, Sam sat on her bed a long time, thinking about what Katy had suggested. She hated it. She thought it had no chance at all of succeeding. And it was dangerous--for both of them, but mostly for Katy.

Sam had been dismayed to learn that at the critical point last night she had "zoned out," leaving Katy defenseless.

"Some back-up," she muttered. "Katy'd be better off hanging garlic around her neck."

She would have put her foot down and refused to participate in this stupid scheme, except that she had no better ideas.

And if it was true, as Katy said, that all day tomorrow Hugh Langford would be at the theater supervising the crews as the sets were disassembled and sent to storage, then tomorrow could be the only chance they had.

Also her mind kept replaying two images over and over: Brianna standing like a mindless wax doll and Mrs. Pye's sad, crumpled, lifeless little body lying on the lineoleum floor. Sam had glimpsed them both just before the metal doors had slammed shut (had *been* slammed shut, she corrected herself); she wished she hadn't.

Sam's eyes filled with tears as they had all day whenever she thought of Mrs. Pye.

"That's not helping," she thought angrily, wiping her eyes with the heels of her hands. She sat on her bed and stared at the floor, trying to analyze what had happened last night.

When had she lost awareness? What had been going on? It seemed to her that there had been *sounds*.... Could that have been what knocked her out? The sounds?

She stood up and make a dash into her parents' bedroom. Her father liked to go the rifle range now and then. In his dresser drawer he kept these odd little wax gizmos. Earplugs.

She found the box and took one out. It didn't look like much of a defense against a demonic force. But she guessed it couldn't hurt. At least it was something.

The box contained four pairs of the wax plugs. She took a pair out, stuck them in the pocket of her jeans, and replaced the box.

Then, with the resilient metabolism of youth, she went down to the kitchen and ate two ham sandwiches and a banana.

"Mom?" Sam called between bites. "There's a slumber party tonight after the show. Do you know where the sleeping bag is?"

Katy's body felt not at all like dancing. She had large bruises rising where she had landed after being thrown out the theater doors, and her muscles felt both weak and knotted.

A hot bath might help. A hot *bubble* bath might even lift her spirits a little, she thought hopefully. Despite what she had said to Sam, she was far from certain that when the moment actually arrived she could find the nerve to put her plan into action.

As the water ran in the tub, she dumped in a triple helping of bath crystals. If at all possible, she wanted to disappear in the foam. The bathroom mirrors gradually fogged, the scent of magnolia and lemon rose in the steam, and Katy slowly lowered herself into the hot, slippery wetness of the bubble bath.

Nijinska, who had a deep-seated mistrust of any body of water larger than a cereal bowl, prowled back and forth on the edge of the tub, now and then patting at Katy's knee where it stuck up out of the water, urging her to "Come out, take my paw, I'll save you!" Katy smiled at the old cat and thought comforting thoughts towards her.

Nijinska stopped her pacing. Her eyes were fixed on a spot in the bath over Katy's submerged stomach. A strange, low yowl rose from her throat, and she began panting rapidly.

Katy looked at the cat in alarm. "Nij? You okay, baby?"

The cat continued her eerie sounds and her rapid, panicky panting. Her fur was rising on her neck and back.

Katy sat up in the bath, looking at the spot in the water that had Nijinska's attention.   Was there something there?   Something under the foam?   She reached out a reluctant hand and slowly cleared the bubbles from a small circle of water.

Words, in a spidery handwriting, floated just below the water's surface.

Crying, Katy beat at the water, smashing her hands into the bubbles, wanting to escape from the tub, escape from the words that followed her even into this private place, escape from this responsibility that she did not want and hadn't asked for...

In a moment, her hands had obliterated most of the foam, but the words still swam peacefully but inexorably in the agitated water. Choking on her angry tears, Katy read,

24 September, 1703
Padua
I have not the strength to write--nor even the courage to recall in full detail--the history of these seven days past.

I am told that the streets of Padua that night rang with my screams, that people closed their shutters against the sounds, and burrowed their ears under pillows, that dogs sped whimpering through the narrow cobbled streets, their hackles raised, fleeing the sound of my voice.

By morning, I lay near death, my voice gone, my bed blood-soaked. I lay in my own gore, my wrists bound to the bedposts with leather straps.

I saw, each time my mind rose through delirium to agonizing pain, the nameless old woman beside me in a wooden chair, eyes closed, chanting fragments of verse as her grey head nodded and swayed rhythmically. Now and again she dipped a bowl of evil-smelling liquid from a kettle simmering on the hearth and bathed my face with it or poured it down my throat until I choked.

Each time the brew touched me, my body contorted and strained against the straps, my lungs pushing ragged, rattling screams through my ruined throat.

I swore a thousand times to kill her the very moment I was freed.

Three days I lay at the mercy of the old gypsy. On the fourth she cut my hands free and helped me to sit and drink a bit of nourishing soup. On the fifth I walked slowly around my bed chamber, leaning heavily on her bony shoulder.

Yesterday I dared to look into my glass. I came to understand this gift she's given me, its workings and its power. It only remains to me to explore the subtle pleasures of its usage.

Today, the seventh day, I rest no more. I go to claim Galina.

ॐ

Even before the words faded in the water, Katy had climbed purposefully out of the tub. As she dried and dressed, what Nijinska felt radiate from her beloved Moon-child was no longer only fear.

The fear was still there, but buried now beneath an avalanche of rage. Her eyes were older, the blue-gray of gun-metal steel, and haunted as soldiers' eyes are before a battle.

Chapter 11:

Langford's New Protogeé

The final performance came and went as
though nothing at all untoward had happened the
night before.

Lise Moreau had apparently recovered fully
from her fainting spell. She danced Snow Queen
with technical brilliance and nothing but
emptiness in her dead green eyes.

Mrs. Pye's duties as costumer were filled by
an efficient, heavy-set woman with frizzy blond
hair named Myra. No reason was given for Myra's
presence or Mrs. Pye's absence.

Katy was so preoccupied with what she was
about to do that she forgot to look for her father at
intermission.   Sam remembered, but didn't
remind her. Katy seemed to have resigned herself
to his absence, and Sam figured she didn't need
the extra stress.

Just before the curtain call, the two friends
held hands in the wings, then hugged each other

with extra intensity before separating, as first Sam, then Katy ran on-stage to bow with the other Soldiers and Snowflakes.

As the curtain closed, Katy took a deep breath and walked straight to Hugh Langford, who was receiving a grateful hug from Brianna.

"Mr. Langford?" Katy said quietly.

Langford turned to her with a cold smile that made it clear he didn't care what, if anything, she had seen and remembered from the night before, that she was powerless to harm him in any way.

"Yes, Miss Moon?" he replied politely, keeping a protective hand on Brianna's shoulder.

"I wanted to thank you for the opportunity of working with you," Katy said, smiling shyly.

Hugh Langford's smile broadened and warmed. "You're quite welcome, Katy. It was my great pleasure to make some small contribution to your dance training."

He removed his hand from Brianna's shoulder and took both Katy's hands in his own, eliciting a small, worried frown from Brianna at the loss of contact.

"I hope," he continued, bowing slightly at the waist and bringing his head down almost level with her own, "I *greatly* hope that I might have that pleasure again very soon. You have a remarkable talent, Katy. I would consider it an honor to participate in its development."

His hands pressed hers delicately, then released to an almost imperceptible lightness, his thumbs gently passing back and forth across the tops of her fingers.

With a deliberate inner mental twist, Katy relinquished all control and let the power of his voice seep into her mind like a drug into her bloodstream. Immediately she felt herself cradled in his care and concern.

Behind his smile lay that sadness distilled over hundreds of years of loneliness--the brilliant artist and teacher who had searched so long for a dancer who could understand his genius and his vision. Who still sought the dancer with a heart and mind and skill to match his own his.

She smiled up into his beautiful face and said, "Brianna tells me that you sometimes take private students. Would you consider taking me?"

Beside them, Brianna's face collapsed.

Langford's eyes searched Katy's, finding there nothing but trust and sincerity, because trust and sincerity was all that was in her mind.

"I will go speak to your mother immediately," he said, as he kissed her lightly on the forehead.

Brianna turned and ran, weeping, from the backstage area. Neither Langford nor Katy noticed her as she went.

"What I should like to suggest," Hugh Langford was saying to Rebecca Moon, "is that she come home with us tonight--" he held up a cautionary hand as Katy's mother looked concerned, "properly chaperoned, of course. She will share a room with Miss Moreau."

Lise Moreau was standing beside him, and smiled on cue. Rebecca looked somewhat reassured, but still objected, "But the day after tomorrow is Christmas Eve..."

"I shall, of course, have her back at your house for your family celebrations," he assured her, waving his hand dismissively. "A studio is no place for a child on Christmas morning.

"But I should like to give her a chance before the first of the year to look the place over, work a few days with me, and decide whether this is really what she wishes to do. We must, after all, finalize our decision before the new school term begins.

"And," he added confidentially, "if she does not wish to accept, we must give Miss Wells time to consider *her* decision. She would be offered the scholarship if Katy declined it. Unless, of course, you wish to decline now..." He looked truly distressed at that possibility, as did Katy.

Rebecca hastened to reassure him. "No, certainly we don't wish to *decline*," she said urgently. "It was just such a surprise! A *wonderful* surprise," she added, touching him lightly on his arm.

"Please, Mom?" Katy begged. "Let me go just for tonight, and tomorrow night? Please? You can come get me before dinner Christmas Eve and that way you can see where I'll be staying..." Katy was almost pleading.

"Oh, Katy," Rebecca sighed. "Christmas Eve? I have all the baking, your Aunt Gina is coming, I still have packages to wrap..."

"I shall be delighted to drive her home myself," Hugh Langford said. He placed his hand on Rebecca's shoulder. "These are small details, Mrs. Moon, which can easily be adjusted to your satisfaction."

"Please, call me Rebecca..." she urged, smiling up at him.

"Of course. Rebecca." Langford's voice was satiny now. "The important things are two-fold: first that your remarkably gifted daughter have the best training available. And second, that you, lovely Rebecca, be completely happy and comfortable with the arrangements. I shall do my sincere best to bring about both."

Rebecca Moon's maternal instincts, a little spotty even on her best days, melted like butter on a hot August sidewalk.

Twenty minutes later, a two-car caravan pulled up at the Moon residence.

While Rebecca served coffee to Hugh Langford and Lise Moreau (who left hers untouched on the end table), Katy dashed upstairs and was throwing toothbrush, dance clothes, and a few odds and ends into a small suitcase when from under the bed came an unearthly, agonized yowl.

"Nij? Come here, girl.." The old cat was invisible in the dark under the bed, except for a baleful green light that burned fiercely in the backs of her retinas. She refused to be coaxed, and Katy had no choice but to leave her alone. She was in a hurry.

"It's okay, Nij," Katy assured her. "I'll only be gone..." Katy paused in confusion, her mind slipping uncomfortably in and out of Langford's influence at this distance. "I'll be back Christmas Eve. Day after tomorrow."

As Katy dragged her suitcase down the stairs, the sound of Nijinska's banshee-like wails followed her down the stairs.

Katy tossed her suitcase into the trunk of Langford's car and kissed her mother and sisters good-bye, leaving an extra kiss behind to be delivered to her father, who was working late. She settled herself happily in the front seat between Lise and Mr. Langford.

Rebecca and the twins stood on the front porch and waved Katy off. As Langford backed the car into the driveway to reverse its direction, an eight-pound streak of fur and fury flew out the open front door toward the car.

Nijinska flung herself at the retreating car and landed atop the trunk. Katy turned in surprise when she heard the "thump," and involuntarily reached back as the car's acceleration slid Nijinska off onto the asphalt.

Rebecca waved them on and grabbed the cat
before she could attack the car again.   Nijinska
twisted out of her grasp, scratching Rebecca
badly, and fled into the bushes.

"Stay there then!" Rebecca muttered, sucking
her hand where it bled. "Stupid cat!"

Chapter 12:

Green Silk

When the car rolled up the long circular drive between Langford's house and the twelve water-elms, it was well past midnight. As they entered, Mr. Langford lit a candelabra and explained to Katy the absence of electric lights.

"I hope you're not too appalled," he apologized. "I assure you we have all the other modern conveniences, including high-speed Internet access."

"It's beautiful," Katy said happily. "I love candles."

"Don't lift that heavy bag, Katy. Miss Moreau will carry it up for you."

Langford, carrying the silver candelabra, led the way up to the fourth-floor. Katy followed behind him.

Lise obediently picked up Katy's bag and came up the steps behind them, but the tension in her shoulders made them draw up toward her ears, giving her a hunched and frightened look.

Langford opened the door to the bed-sitting room, and Katy could hardly keep from jumping up and down in delight. At the far end of the room was a massive four-poster bed with a forest green silk canopy. The lustrous fabric was pulled into the center of the canopy frame where it bunched into a ruffled medallion. The bedspread and pillow shams were the same rich green silk. The spread had been turned for the night, and Katy could see that the sheets were a much paler shade of green, in an even finer silk. The bed was stacked so high with mattresses that a small brocade foot-stool was required to climb into it.

As Katy turned around in wonder in the center of the room, Lise struggled up the last stair-step and stood in the doorway, not putting the bag down.

In a low, barely audible tone Lise said, "This is *my* room."

Hugh Langford turned to her, his face a stainless steel mask. "You are mistaken, my dear. This room, indeed all the rooms in this house, are mine."

Lise's eyes grew narrow and speculative. She still did not put the bag down.

Langford held out his hand imperiously, and after a pause, she gave him the suitcase. Under his stare, she dropped her eyes to the floor.

He placed Katy's suitcase beside a large mahogany chest of drawers with a marble top. Turning back to Katy, he said apologetically, "You'll have to share the bed, I'm afraid. But only for a short while. Miss Moreau will be making other arrangements."

The ballerina turned quickly and walked out of the room, as if in anger. Katy struggled to recall something about Lise--something Lise had told her. She seemed to recall seeing her on the floor, her tiara beside her head... had she fallen? Katy couldn't remember. It didn't seem important anymore.

So this would be her new home! Incredible.

As Mr. Langford lit a candle for Katy from his own, he asked, "So, Katy?   Will you be comfortable here, do you think?"

"Oh, yes!" breathed Katy. "It's perfect!"

"Then I'll leave you to unpack. There is a bathroom through that door. Ask Miss Moreau for anything else you need."

He started out the door, then turned back into the room, leaning with elegant ease against the doorjamb, the candlelight flickering warmly around him.

"Oh, and tomorrow? Sleep as late as you like, Katy. I must spend most of the day at the Opera House seeing to the striking of the set and the storage of the costumes..."

At the word "costumes," something that might have been doubt flickered across his face and then passed.

"I'd like for you to give yourself a barre before I get back tomorrow afternoon--you need to focus particularly on your turn-out, please--and we will work some together after dinner. Does that suit you?"

Katy smiled the bright smile of a girl whose wildest fantasy has been suddenly become solid reality. "That suits me perfectly, thank you, Mr. Langford. Thank you for everything!"

He returned her smile, lifted a strand of her hair in his fingers, and said with strange choking intensity, "I want very badly to see you dance for me, Katy. I *need* to see you dance for me."

He backed slowly away from her, and she heard his soft footsteps becoming even softer and then disappearing as he descended the staircase.

It took Katy only two minutes to put away her few things in an empty drawer. Then she went into the bathroom, showered, brushed her teeth, and put on the floor-length nightgown she had brought to sleep in instead of her big T-shirt.

At the opposite end of the room from the bed was a delicate game table with a green leather top. Beside it was a gilt chair, the only one in the room. In obedience to a sudden impulse, Katy took her single candle, placed it on the table, and seated herself in the chair.

She sat still and silent, in unconscious imitation of how Lise Moreau had sat there night after endless night for all the years since she had come there at the age of ten.

Eventually her eyes started to close of their own volition. She got up, climbed up into the huge bed, and nestled down into the unaccustomed feel of real silk sheets. She blew out her candle and let herself drift off toward sleep.

Just before she fell asleep, the last thing she was aware of was that Lise had come back into the room in the dark. Katy could see her in the moonlight, and moved over to provide enough room in the bed.

Lise, however, walked instead to the little gilt chair and sat down. She was still sitting there in the moonlight and the stillness when Katy's eyes closed.

❦

As the moon began its long descent, its reflection in the lake was crossed by the pale shadow of an owl winging toward the house. The owl paused briefly in one of the twelve water elms, then in a long silent arc came to light on the balcony rail outside the bedroom where Katy slept.

In the graceful circular driveway that divided the house from the trees, the back door of Hugh Langford's car opened with a soft "snick" sound. Out of the back seat crept a small figure with boy-cut hair.

Chapter 13:

Inside

Katy did indeed sleep late the next morning. She awoke alone tangled in green silk with a vague feeling that at one point Lise had come to bed, but she had no clear memory of it.

Her first sensation on opening her eyes was one of perfect happiness, but now that she was no longer near Hugh Langford, his hold over her thought process evaporated, taking her peace of mind with it.

Slowly she forced herself to mentally brush away the remaining wisps of his effect on her and painfully reconstructed her true memories of Mrs. Pye and Lise and Brianna. As she called those memories, they came slinking back to her dragging a blanket of fear that settled over her like a shroud.

She climbed out of the big bed, found her jeans and a sweater in the dresser where she had carefully unpacked them, dressed, and headed downstairs carrying her coat. Somewhere on the property she knew--she hoped--Sam would have hidden herself away. And unless she had managed to sneak into the house, she was going to be one cold popsicle of a kid.

She saw no sign of anyone as she came downstairs into the great entryway. She found the kitchen--and a note from Langford reminding her that he and Lise had gone to the theater and would be back in the late afternoon. She was invited to make herself at home and help herself to anything in the kitchen. The note closed with specific instructions about turn-out exercises which made her wrinkle her nose in disgust. Apparently even if you sold your soul, there was no escaping this turn-out thing.

She was starved, but she couldn't go rummaging through the refrigerator until she had found Sam. After that, however, she planned to eat pretty much non-stop for an hour or two.

There was a back door leading from the kitchen to a laundry room with painted wooden walls, and from there to the back of the property. She went out that way, checking to make sure that the door wouldn't lock behind her. The back yard was not fenced, just an open area that eventually merged with a dirt road and then some cultivated fields further on.

About 50 yards from the house were a couple of storage sheds, and Katy thought that those were a likely place for Sam to have holed up for the night. She called her friend's name softly as she walked toward them.

A thin layer of crusty snow made a crunching sound as she walked. She approached the closest shed and heard a crunch that didn't come from her own feet.

"Sam?" she called.

From behind the shed something that looked like a lumpy pile of abandoned tarps lifted one of it's ends: Sam's head.

"K-K-Katy?" came back a small, miserable voice. "I'm s-s-s-so co-old!"

Katy ran to her and hugged her, rubbing her arms to try to get some circulation going again. "Are you okay? You must be frozen!"

In spite of Katy's genuine concern, she had to struggle to keep from laughing. Sam was right out of Dickens--a miserable, pathetic little rag-child.

"All I could find in a hurry was this st-stupid summer sleeping b-bag. And... and... my ears are freezing... and I kept wanting to cry but I was afraid my tears would freeze and give me frost bite. Look at me! I'm blue! And I hate this and I hate *you* and I want to go home and if you don't get me inside in the next ten seconds I am never going to be your friend again *as long as you live!*"

Katy's laughter was out of control now, and Sam glared at her with murder in her eyes. "Which won't be long," she promised darkly.

Thirty minutes later both girls were once again warm and well-fed, having made deep dents in the contents of the well-stocked refrigerator. Sam's sulk was still in evidence, but it had started to take on the characteristics of a running gag, and Katy felt free to ignore it.

Between bites, Sam was giving a truly deadly impression of Katy Moon, Heroine/Cheerleader.

"'Okay, I've got like this really great idea, okay? We'll both go to Hugh Langford's house and, like, risk our lives trying to keep him from

sucking the souls out of little girls, okay? Oh!
Oh! But, see, like, we should do something really
cool, like, see, one of us--*you!*--can sleep, like, in
the *snow!* Behind this really gross old outhouse!
With, like, rats and stuff crawling all over you!
And how cool would *that* be!?!'"

Katy sighed and patted Sam's hand as an
adult would a small, fussy child. "There were no
rats."

"Oh yeah? And how would you know there
were no rats? You were tucked away in a four-
poster bed with silk sheets! *Green* silk sheets!"
For some reason Sam felt more affronted by Katy's
bedding than anything else.

Katy arched one winged eyebrow. "Too cold
for rats." She popped the last bite of toast and
marmalade into her mouth and got up from the
table.

Sam looked around her at the old-fashioned
kitchen with its wood and copper and ceramic tile.
"This place is enormous. Who do you suppose
does the cleaning?"

At her house, Sam's part of the chores
included the non-carpeted floors; large expanses
of hardwood and tile always drew her attention.

"Gnomes," replied Katy. "Met 'em last night.
They sleep in the cellar."

"Lucky gnomes. Cellars are lot warmer than
outside. Behind the outhouse. Where *I* slept.
With the rats." She held up a hand to forestall
Katy's objection. "In their tiny little down-filled
rat-parkas. And mittens. *They* had mittens."

"If I could interrupt your pity party for a
moment, we should get to work."

"Ah, yes," sighed Sam, "the enchanted shoes.
When your brain had this little chat with Lise's
brain, did she by any chance mention where the
enchanted shoe closet *was*?"

"Think of it as a computer game," Katy said
airily. "We just have to search the castle from
turret to gnome-infested cellar."

"I hate those games," pouted Sam. "I always
get killed in about two seconds. How many lives
do you figure we have?"

"One each," Katy cautioned her. "So don't
screw up. Do you want to start on the top floor or
the bottom?"

"I *don't* want to start. I want to go home and
stay there. But if you insist, I guess the bottom.
Is there a basement?"

"No idea. But probably the logical place for a
cellar door would be either in the kitchen or
outside. I don't see one in the kitchen."

"Oh, man!" Sam whined. "I don't want to go
outside again! You go and report back."

"Not a chance, Boy Wonder.   Button up."
Katy pushed the reluctant Sam through the utility
room and out the back door.

Chapter 14:

The Villains
Always Get the Great Houses

There was, in fact, a door on the side of the house leading down into the cellar. It was not locked, and they were able to see down the steps into the single room below. It was dusty and cobwebby. It was also completely empty. No doors or windows or openings of any kind interrupted the blank concrete uniformity of the walls.

"Who has a basement with nothing in it? Literally, nothing?" Sam asked rhetorically.

"Well, it's a big house," said Katy. "And maybe out in the country like this, people keep their basement stuff in the sheds."

They walked out to the two storage sheds. Both sheds were unlocked. Both were as empty as the cellar.

"So why didn't you sleep in here?" Katy asked as they stared into the empty space.

"Because I couldn't *see* in there," Sam replied. "Snakes and spiders live in sheds."

"And that's worse than rats?"

"The bigger, tougher rats stay in the sheds. It's the smaller, wimpy rats who get thrown outside by the big rats."

"Anyway, there's nothing here. Let's go back in."

Back in the house, they explored the first floor. The house faced almost directly south, and the kitchen with its small utility room occupied its north-west corner.

Downstairs, in addition to the kitchen, there was the formal entry with its staircase rising in a splendid curve and three large rooms: dining room on the south west corner, a library on the north east, and a room opposite the dining room across the entryway that in Katy's house was called the living room, but which in this house they could only think of as "the parlor." There was also a small powder room off the entryway.

They looked quickly through the kitchen cupboards and pantry, which contained only normal kitchen equipment and supplies. Sam opened a small sliding panel in the north wall and saw behind it an open shaft and a network of ropes and pulleys. "Hey, what's this?" she called.

"Neat!" Katy exclaimed, coming to join her. "That's a dumb waiter. I've never seen one before."

"But what *is* it?" Sam repeated.

"Sort of a little freight elevator that you work by hand. They used them to send things like trays of food up to the upper floors. For the ladies when they were having a fit of the vapors." She brought the back of one hand to her head in a fainting gesture. "That way the maid didn't have to carry things up and down the stairs. You pull on the rope and there's sort of a box-thing that comes down."

Sam pulled on the rope experimentally, but it wouldn't budge. "Must be broken."

"Okay.   Nothing in the kitchen except food and dishes," Katy concluded. "Moving on."

"The dining room's easy," observed Sam as they walked through it. "Just a big table and a couple of corner cabinets.   No place to hide anything like twelve pairs of shoes."

"Pretty, though," Katy said, wistfully running her fingers down the gleaming cherry-wood banquet table. She loved antiques, and this was very close to being her dream house.

They crossed through the foyer on the way to the parlor, peeking in the door of the powder room as they passed it.

Two bronze sculptures of young ballerinas stood on marble pedestals at the foot of the staircase. To the left of the stairs, a dancer sat in a wide second position, dance bag beside her, holding a single pointe shoe in her hands. One foot was bare, and the strap of her camisole leotard dropped off one shoulder. The sculpture was titled "New Shoes," and had an intimate, vulnerable, but tranquil quality about it.

The second sculpture was much more dramatic: a dancer upside down in mid-lift, her partner's hand in the small of her back, his muscular arm descending to a swirled base. The lift was one that Katy had not done yet; it looked both scary and thrilling and made her toes tingle a little like looking over the edge of a high cliff.

"You gotta admit," Sam observed, peering carefully at the sculptures, "the guy has taste."

The girls moved on to the parlor, which was furnished with a lovely settee and matching chairs, upholstered in wine-colored raw silk, the wood of the arms and legs polished to a soft glow. There were also a pair of matching campaign chests with brass corners and a tall, elaborately carved armoire. The girls opened all three pieces and found them empty. Nothing else in the room could be used for storage.

Double French doors connected the parlor with Langford's library. The library was at the back of the house, tucked behind the staircase. It was the smallest room downstairs. On his mahogany desk lay seven or eight pieces of paper, and the bookshelves were filled with leather-bound volumes and small sculptures.

"Finally! Stuff!" muttered Sam, starting to dig through the desk drawers.

"Stuff, but no shoes," Katy concluded fifteen minutes later when they had combed through every drawer and cabinet.

"Upstairs," directed Sam. They headed back through the living room to the staircase. As they ascended, Sam looked critically at the strip of thick carpet that ran up the middle two-thirds of the stairsteps, leaving a wide margin of exposed wood on either side.

"This is the worst," she declared. "Thick carpet *and* wood--on steps. You can vacuum them both, but it takes two different settings on the machine, and you have to drag it up and down the steps, and..."

"That," explained Katy, "is why he has all those gnomes. Get over it, Sam. You don't have to clean it. Second floor."

Sam whistled through her teeth as they stepped onto the second floor landing. "Wow! What's this?"

"Don't know. I saw it when I came down this morning, but I didn't stop to check it out."

A broad empty hallway ran the entire width of the house, and there was only a single door in the wall that faced them.

They opened it slowly, and saw that it was windowless and too dark to enter without a light. Katy picked up a candelabra and matches from the landing, explaining to Sam that Langford had an aversion to electric lights.

"I knew it!" Sam cried. "He's a vampire! They can't be seen in electric lights or something."

"You're thinking about mirrors. Vampires don't cast a reflection in *mirrors*. And that would be a real problem for a vampire that taught ballet, wouldn't it?"

"Oh. Right. Never mind."

Behind the single second-floor door was Hugh Langford's private theater. By the light of the candelabra they saw the curtained stage, with its single armchair in the center of the audience.

"Very, very creepy," Sam whispered. Katy didn't speak.

They walked slowly and cautiously around the windowless room, past three more large bronze sculptures of dancers, both of them nervous as cats and jumping at the shadows of the bronzes the candlelight cast on the walls.

Sam walked up the steps that led to the stage, pulled aside a corner of the heavy black velvet curtain, and was stepping behind it when she realized that Katy had halted.

"You okay, kid?"

"I... I can't go up there," Katy stammered. "I can't." She was trembling.

Sam came quickly back down the three steps and touched her arm. "What is it?"

"That... that's where..." she started backing away from the stage, shaking her head violently from side to side. "That's where he takes them.

He makes them dance there, and he... he takes them..."

"Takes what, Katy?"

"*Them*!!! He takes *them*! Who they are! He watches while they dance, and the part of them that is their *selves* gets sucked out of them and into him. This is where he does it, Sam! I can't go up there! I can't!!!"

Katy was near hysterics now, and Sam had to lead her out of the theater to calm her down.

"Okay, Katy, shhhh... It's okay. You don't have to."

In the sunlight of the landing, Katy grew quieter, but tears were streaming down her face. "I'm sorry, Sam. I just couldn't."

"No problem, all right? I can go. You don't have to. Do you think you'll be okay here by yourself for a couple of minutes? Just long enough for me to check what's back there?" Katy nodded mutely. "You sure?" Another nod. "Then wait right here. I'll be as quick as I can."

Sam took the candelabra from Katy's hand and went back into the dark theater. Even Sam, who didn't have Katy's sensitivity, found the room sinister, particularly in the candlelight which sank into the black velvet and disappeared.

The chair for one viewer disturbed her most of all. Sam had discovered that she enjoyed performing. She was already able to establish a connection between herself and the audience, sensing their response to her movements on-stage, and it gave her a sense of power.

But dancing here, she knew, would feel completely different. Like being spied on in a private moment and at the same time being aware of it but unable to stop it. Unwholesome. Nasty.

Behind the black velvet drapes she found an empty stage, the chandeliers suspended above the stage and the foot-light candles at its front edge. In the wings were nothing but the controls for opening the curtains and starting the music.

Sam was anxious to get out of there, but she forced herself to search carefully behind the endless folds of velvet draperies until she was sure she hadn't missed anything.

Relieved, she hurried back out to the hallway where Katy sat huddled on the stairs waiting.

"Nothing back there," Sam reported briskly. "Next floor."

From the second floor, the staircase rose to a small windowed landing at the front of the house, then turned ninety degrees and rose to the third floor. Above the second floor it became narrower and darker, so they kept the candelabra.

Where the stairwell opened onto the third-floor landing, the girls found themselves with a choice of three doors. Directly facing them on the north was a modest bathroom. It contained an assortment of men's toiletries and linens. Nothing more.

The door to the left of the staircase opened into a small windowless room on the west side of the house, furnished with an antique sleighbed, a highboy chest of drawers, a small writing desk with a chair, and a bedside table with a lamp and a book.

This was Hugh Langford's room, and Katy was careful not to touch anything of his. Sam picked up the book. It was a biography of Diaghilev. There was no bookmark in it.

At the south end of the room was a small closet containing neatly hung men's clothing; highly polished men's shoes were laid in a precise row on the floor. Sam rifled quickly through the immaculate clothes.

"Make sure you don't re-arrange anything," Katy urged.

"Yeah," agreed Sam. "This guy is so obsessive- compulsive he probably color-codes his sock drawer."

A search of the highboy revealed only neatly folded clothes.

"What did I tell you?" Sam exclaimed, standing on tip-toe to peek into the top drawer. Katy saw over her shoulder that his socks were rolled in tight coils, a row of black socks, a row of brown, a row of navy.

Since this room was on the same side of the house as the kitchen, on the north wall, next to the desk, was the dumb-waiter. Sam slid the door aside, and behind it was the plain wooden box that had once raised and lowered dinner trays or laundry baskets to the kitchen. It was empty.

"I don't think there's anything here. Let's go," urged Katy. The smell of Langford's expensive dry cologne was disturbing her.

They crossed the hall to the east room. It was quite a bit larger than Langford's and empty, containing no furniture at all, not even an area rug on the bare floor. The closet was also empty. There were no drapes on the two windows.

"Again, no stuff," Sam muttered. "How do you get to be that old and not have any stuff?"

"There was some stuff. In the kitchen. The library. Bathroom stuff in the bathroom. His clothes in the bedroom."

"But it's all just rented-room stuff," Sam objected. "Stuff you'd bring with you if you were going on a long trip. Open any drawer at my house, and you find junk. Old odds and ends. Buttons and pennies and grocery lists and little plastic pieces that you know go to something but you can't remember what. Even in the office there was nothing *extra*, you know what I mean? Exactly the papers he needed, but no junk mail, no scrap of paper with just a phone number on it. One nice pen in the drawer, but no paper clips or rubber bands. Not so much as a deck of cards. Anywhere!"

"So he's neat, Sam, I don't see..."

"No, not neat. Neat is when all the papers on the desk are in one nice stack with a paperweight on top. His were scattered around. It's like a movie set, Katy. Like this is all placed here so it will look like a normal person living a normal life. Props. But a normal person accumulates too many things in his life to have completely empty sheds and basements and rooms or even drawers."

"So what does that mean?"

The two girls looked at each other for a long time. Then Sam shrugged. "I have no idea. Try the next floor."

The last stairs were darker and narrower still. At their top the girls saw the same arrangement of doors they had encountered on the third floor.

"That's my room," Katy said, pointing to the left. "And that's the bathroom straight ahead. Start with the other room."

Like the one below it on the third floor, the east room was empty, with two windows looking out over a gently rolling countryside. "Nice view," observed Sam.

"The one in my room is even better, Katy said. "And there's a balcony."

"Well, let's go check it out. There's nothing in here."

The view was indeed lovely. On this side of the house, the terrain fell away in a gentle slope to a creekbed that fed the lake in front of the house. Behind the creek rose a dark woods. No neighboring farms or houses were visible for a long distance. Sam and Katy searched the room thoroughly and then allowed themselves a short rest, leaning against the doorjamb of the balcony.

"Villains always get the great houses, don't they?" Katy observed.

"Like who?"

"Oh you know--Dracula, Frankenstein, the witch in 'Hansel and Gretel,' the Beast in 'Beauty and the Beast.'"

"Yeah, but there's also the Batcave and Superman's Fortress of Solitude. It's not just the villains. *Everybody* lives better than we do. Come on, we're almost done."

The only door left was the bathroom, and it was no more shoe-filled than the rest of the house. They looked around at the ceilings, trying to find a trap door that might lead to another attic space, but the ceilings were featureless except for their plaster moldings.

"Now what?" asked Sam.

Katy sighed. "I don't know. Start over?"

"I don't see what good that would do. There's just nothing." They were standing in the central open space by the stairs, and Sam took one last look in all three rooms. "Funny how he furnished just the west bedrooms. The ones on the east are so much larger."

"My room has the balcony. They're about the same size if you count that."

"But on the third floor..." The two girls exchanged raised-eyebrow looks.

"Bring the candles," directed Katy as she headed for the stairs.

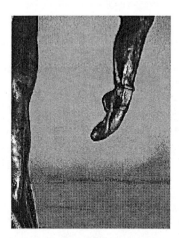

Chapter 15:

A Room with No View

Back in Hugh Langford's bedroom they stood looking at the windowless west wall. The room was only half the width of the empty east bedroom, and even with only the few pieces of furniture, it looked cramped.

"So the lord of the manor," mused Sam, "chooses the smallest bedroom, the only one with no windows and no view, leaves two bigger, nicer ones others unfurnished, and gives the very best one with the great view *and* a balcony, to his zombie victim. Not exactly in character, is it?"

"Don't call her a zombie," Katy admonished. "The next zombie could be me."

"Whatever. The point is, this is not the room you'd expect him to take. The other point is, there's no reason for this room to be so small. It should be as big as your room plus the balcony, right? Everything else on these two floors is the same--even the bathrooms. There's a space missing, and it's exactly the size and shape of the balcony upstairs. And it's gotta be behind that wall."

"So how do you get to it?" Katy puzzled, busily feeling around the wall, alternately pushing and knocking on it with her knuckles. "It's just flat sheetrock. I don't see a crack or a panel or anything that could be a secret door."

Sam stood leaning against the opposite wall, doing nothing at all. Katy turned to her in exasperation. "Would you please help a little?"

Sam shrugged. "I don't see any point banging on it. My dad does that when he looks for a stud in the wall to hang a picture. He knocks around for ten minutes, then he gets this 'Ah hah!' look on his face and hammers in the nail. So far he's been wrong 100% of the time. I don't expect I'd do any better."

Katy stood with her hands on her hips, "So what do you suggest?"

"Gimme a minute, okay?" Sam's eyes were traveling around the room. At one point she peeled up the edge of the oriental rug closest to the west wall. The floor was as featureless as the sheetrock.

Then her eyes lit on the small square door of the dumbwaiter. It was chest-high in the north wall, its right-hand edge against the bathroom wall directly to the east of it. "There," Sam announced authoritatively. "That's how you get in."

Katy looked skeptical. "It's on the wrong side of the room."

"Probably a tunnel through the north wall. Like a little hallway."

Katy slid open the door. The wooden box that served as the elevator cage seemed solid and unmoveable. "Well, if it's through here, it must be behind this. Didn't we decide it was stuck?"

Sam joined her now. The two of them pushed and rattled the box in its shaft. They pulled on the ropes, but the box didn't budge up or down. They searched the mechanism for clamps or pins that would stop the ropes from moving.

After about five minutes of this, the girls were both sweaty and frustrated, and Sam plopped down on the sleigh-bed while Katy stood in the middle of the room, both of them breathing heavily and staring glumly at the dumb-waiter.

"I still think I'm right," Sam said slowly. "It's gotta be through there.   There's probably an opening in the north wall that runs from the left of the box into the space behind the west wall. But how does he move the box?"

Katy paced. She was feeling pitifully under-skilled for this sort of detective work.

Sam let herself fall backwards across the bed, her feet still on the floor, her arms flung over her head. With her body extended sideways across the bed, she fiddled with the cord to the lamp on the bedside table. The lamp had a fussy little satin shade with gold braid and tassels--a grandmotherly sort of dressing table lamp. It made Katy giggle a little to think of evil Hugh Langford turning on this silly...

Suddenly Katy stopped pacing and pointed toward Sam's hands. "Sam? There's a lamp on that table!"

"Swell, Katy. And there's a chair by the desk. Just a sec. I'm thinking."

Katy grabbed Sam's legs insistently and bounced her up and down. "A lamp, Sam! He doesn't allow electric lights in his house, remember? What's a lamp doing on his bedside table?"

Now she had Sam's attention. The two of
them stared closely at the little lamp. "There's no
light bulb," observed Sam.

"But it's plugged in." Katy walked around the
bed and reached slowly for the little chain that
hung from the socket. She looked at Sam, who
nodded, then pulled it gently.

Behind them, in the north wall, the box of the
dumb-waiter slid silently down three feet and
stopped, exposing the walls of the shaft.

Katy pulled the chain again. The box
returned to its original position. A third pull on
the chain, and the box slid down again.

From where they were, the girls could not see
the left side of the shaft, and they walked slowly,
cautiously over to the dumb-waiter, reaching
reflexively for each other's hands as they
approached the dark empty hole that opened
exactly where Sam had claimed it must.

Chapter 16:

Behind the Walls

Katy found it disturbingly reminiscent of the hole behind Hugh Langford's eyepatch. She half expected to see fog come creeping out at her.

Sam swallowed hard and said, "So I guess we should go in, huh?"

Katy peered into the absolute black of the little tunnel. "I guess. But we better go now because in about two seconds I'm going to chicken out."

She boosted herself up into the opening, sitting on the top of the wooden box which was now hidden in the wall. "Hand me the candelabra," she told Sam, who did.

Still sitting on the dumb-waiter, Katy moved the silver candlestick into the opening, looking at the walls of the tunnel. It was no more than two feet wide. She couldn't see very far in front of her, but there were exposed wall studs supporting the house's exterior wood siding to her right, bare wooden studs and sheetrock to her left, all of it furry with cobwebs and dust. The tunnel itself, however, was relatively clear of cobwebs, as though someone passed through it regularly.

She turned back around to Sam, pried one of the candles out, and handed the candelabra back to her. "You were right. It's a little hallway. But it's really narrow, so we'd better just take one candle each so we don't set fire to the house."

With one candle held in her hand, Katy swung her legs over the edge of the dumb-waiter and dropped into the tunnel. As she crept along the corridor, her candle made little sizzling sounds each time it brushed a spider web.

Sam watched Katy disappear into the hole, then took a candle for herself and followed her.

The tunnel was no more than ten feet in length, but in the inky darkness, moving one foot tentatively after the other, watching nervously for spiders and guarding the candle flames so they didn't touch the walls, it seemed to go on forever.

When they reached the end, Katy stopped and drew a deep breath, steeling herself for whatever she might find as the dark space opened to her left into a larger room.

"Hey, Katy?" came Sam's voice weakly behind her. "You know in those horror movies how stupid it always seems when the girl goes out alone to investigate the weird noise she hears, even after she knows that something has killed about fifty of her friends? Does this feel at all like that to you?"

"This feels *exactly* like that to me," Katy replied. "What's your point?"

"No point," said Sam. "Just thought I'd mention it. In case you wanted to rethink anything."

In front of her, Katy stepped around the corner into the greater darkness. As the feeble light of her candle reached uncertainly into the gloom, Katy saw stretching out before her a long narrow room, perhaps six feet wide by twenty feet long. It must, she thought, run the whole depth of the house, including the staircase.

At the room's approximate mid-point, its back against the outside wall, squatted a large roll-top desk. Papers were scattered across its surface and stuffed into all its cubbyholes. On the floor beside it were stacks of papers and notebooks, and one of the stacks had collapsed onto the floor. Four large filing cabinets also had stacks of paper on them. One of the drawers stood open, and it was packed to overflowing with file folders.

Rough, unpainted boards attached to the wall served as shelves. On the shelves stood long rows of slender bound volumes. Journals. Hundreds of journals.

"Sam?" Katy called. "Here's the stuff."

There were no shoes in the room, but at the far end of the space a square hole in the floor opened into a dark pit. A clumsily constructed wooden ladder led downwards and out of sight.

Katy walked to the edge of the opening and stood looking down into the dark, her heart in her throat. A smell of mildew and incense rose out of the dark toward her. Beneath those smells was another, something sour that smelled like fear.

Behind her, Sam couldn't resist taking down one of the journals and leafing through it.

"Oh, man!" she exclaimed. "This one was written during the First World War! In Uruguay! Figures," she sniffed. "He sat out the war and probably cleaned up on the black market."

She replaced the volume and took down an older one. "This one is from..." She looked up in shock. "1724."

Sam flipped through the pages until a name caught her eye. She swallowed hard, cleared her throat, and read,

"3 April

Langford Estate, England

"The game warden made a grim discovery today. Where the snows are newly melted at the wood's edge, he came upon Galina's body in the stream bed, her feet bare, her long black hair tangled to her waist, her once-lovely throat torn out by the wolves that prowl the estate in deep winter.

"When I turned her out this twelve-months past, she took to roam the countryside, a mindless animal, dancing and singing alone on the heath at midnight, begging for scraps from the kitchen maids.

"When winter came and she howled no more beneath my window in the full of the moon, I was relieved to be shut of the creature. It is indeed good news that I shall be allowed to enjoy the fine spring weather without the annoyance of an aging madwoman at my elbow."

Sam looked up from the page, trying to grasp the reality of the book she held in her hand.

"It's all true..." she muttered. "It's all actually true." She quickly replaced the volume and took out the next.

"Sam..." Katy started to object.

"Yeah, I know. I'm coming. Just one more.

"6 June," she read, *"Dublin, Ireland*

"I saw a most extraordinary child today: a lovely pink-cheeked lass dancing clever jigs with shy eyes and nimble feet at the County Fair. I spoke straight off to her father, whether she might not like dancing better in a velvet gown with pearls

about her throat; he seems quite content to take the purse I offered and save her keep at his table.

"If she will serve, I shall cut short my travels and return with my new prize to my estates. I am most eager for a remedy to these grey hairs that come so quickly, these lines about my mouth that deepen daily.

"And she is lovely, in truth. The thought of her, her image in my mind, stirs feelings I had near forgot. I'll have her portrait done, perhaps, and hang it next Galina's."

"That's enough!" Katy snapped. "It scares me. And we still don't have any shoes."

"It's fascinating, Katy. Absolutely obscene, but fascinating. If we actually get rid of him, I *want* these journals. For the first time I get why people become historians; when you think that he actually wrote these things as they happened..."

"You're welcome to them, trust me. But first we need shoes. And Sam? I think they're down here."

Chapter 17:

Down the Rabbit Hole

The two stood close together for several seconds, smelling the strange air that drafted up, each wishing the other would change her mind.

Katy knelt down on the floor. "Alice down the rabbit hole," she muttered as she stepped onto the first rung.

"Curioser and curioser," Sam added as she followed Katy into the blackness.

The ladder descended fifteen or twenty feet to a second room, the same size and shape as the one they had just left.

"So where are we?" Katy muttered as she stepped off the last rung onto a solid wood floor.

"This has to be still on the west end of the house, but on the second floor. We're probably behind the stage in that creepy theater."

In the light of their candles, the girls could make out a line of small pedestals, like little altars, which stood arranged down both sides of the room.

On each pedestal was a pair of shoes.

Katy held her candle up in front of the first one. It held a pair of child-sized ballet slippers, scuffed and worn, the shape of the little toes still imprinted in the soft leather that had been fitted tightly and stretched over the foot.

Sam was by her side now, holding her candle up so that its light fell on the wall behind the pedestal. On the wall was a color photograph in a heavy frame. The picture was of a size and quality usually associated with formal wedding portraits.

A brown-haired child in a peach-colored leotard and pink tights. A ten-year-old Lise Moreau. She stood in the center of an empty studio, staring out at the viewer as though staring at her reflection in the mirror. Behind her, also looking intently at her imagined reflection as he adjusted the position of her arms, was Hugh Langford. The girl's expression was one of intense concentration, tinged with the slight dissatisfaction a dancer always feels looking at the imperfectability of her body.

From Langford's face, however, shone the pride and possessiveness of the teacher of a brilliant student. A word echoed in Katy's mind, one she had never quite understood before: covet.

Across from Lise's pedestal was a similar arrangement of shoes and portrait. Hugh Langford with another child, another studio.

Then a third similar portrait. From Langford's clothing, Katy guessed that one had been taken in the 1960's, the other, which was hand-tinted, in perhaps the 30's.

The fourth portrait, also hand-tinted, was of Langford with a slightly older girl, dressed in a modern adaptation of a Greek toga. It reminded

Katy of pictures she had seen of Isadora Duncan's students taken in the early 1900's. The girl wore sandals laced high up her legs, the same sandals that lay on the pedestal below the photograph. Langford sat beside her in a chair, one hand protectively around her waist, posed formally for the camera. He wore a suit with a high-necked vest and a high, stiff-collared shirt. Other than his old-fashioned attire, he looked exactly the same.

Sam whistled softly. "Katy, he really *is* that old!"

"Yeah," Katy agreed, "it's one thing to read it on paper, but it's really something else to *see* it, isn't it?"

Next came a series portraits with young girls in a variety of folk-dance costumes: an old tintype photograph on a thin metal plate of Langford with a child in a heavily embroidered dress and an odd hat; a pen-and-ink drawing of Langford with a girl in a Polynesian-style sarong; a carefully executed watercolor of him with a Native American child in beaded deerskin.

Of the last portraits, three included no likeness of Langford. Above a pair of grass ankle bracelets, instead of a painting or a photograph, a small clay sculpture of an African child sat on a semi-circular shelf. Another pair of ankle bracelets, these with tiny bells, lay below a wooden sculpture of an East Indian girl. On a rice-paper scroll in Chinese ink was a drawing of a young girl dancing with a feather fan; her shoes were embroidered silk.

Then came an oil painting of Langford and a fair-haired girl dressed in a blue gown to match her eyes. They were seated in a room that looked like an old English castle.

"He gets around, doesn't he?" Katy observed.

"Obviously," explained Sam, veteran horror-story reader, "he has to 'die' every so often, pack up his money, and start another life in a new country."

At the end of the line of pedestals, above an ancient pair of leather slippers, hung another oil portrait, superbly executed, of a dark-eyed child whose black curls spilled over her shoulders and down to her waist. She wore a pale velvet gown embroidered with seed pearls and sat in a carved wooden chair. Her red leather slippers did not reach the floor.

Langford sprawled at her feet in languid elegance, propped by one elbow on a pile of cushions. The girl's empty, hopeless eyes stared blankly out at the artist, but Langford smiled with private satisfaction up at the girl. His hand was closed around one of her delicate ankles like a shackle.

"Galina," Katy whispered.

They paused before this portrait and the faded red slippers, thinking of the child whose living feet had danced in them, whose living ankle had been held by the man with the patch.

They had now passed down the entire room, past twelve pedestals. At the very end of the room stood a thirteenth.

Katy reached for Sam's hand as she lifted her candle to it. There were no shoes on this pedestal (yet), but above it a black and white photograph had been thumb-tacked in place: a snapshot taken backstage of a young ballerina in a beaded white tutu waiting in the wings to make her entrance, the available light from the brightly lit stage illuminating her eyes which sparked with excitement. Katy Moon.

On the floor in front of it, as though hurriedly torn from the wall, lay a discarded photograph of Brianna Wells.

Chapter 18:

Call Us, and We Will Come

Katy was shaken to her core by the sight of her own photograph--a photograph which he had obviously taken even before she asked to become his student.

He had taken her picture without her permission or even her knowledge! As though he had *fantasized* about her! She felt sick and terrified. And she felt furious. She reached out and ripped the picture from the wall.

"Not me, Hugh Langford," she swore under her breath. "Not me. Come on, Sam, get the shoes. I'd better not touch them. I don't want to zone out."

Twelve pairs of shoes is a lot to carry. After some discussion, they went back up the ladder and scrounged a pillow case from the linen closet

in the bathroom.   Then they returned to the
hidden room and dumped the shoes into the
pillow case.

They left through the dumb-waiter, returning
its secret door to its closed position using the
lamp mechanism.

Before they left Langford's bedroom, they
smoothed over the bed where they had been
sitting on it and checked the room carefully to
make sure they hadn't left any other traces of
their visit behind.

"Next, the elm trees," Katy directed, heading
for the stairs with Sam close behind her lugging
the shoes.   She glanced at a clock on Langford's
dresser.   "We'd better hurry.   It's later than I
thought.   His note said he'd be back late
afternoon, and it's already 4:00."

The twelve old trees stood leafless and dark
between the house and the lake, their trunks
almost black against the frosted landscape.   The
elms did not exactly make a circle, more, as Sam
observed, like an amoeba trying to leave in three
different directions.   But they did effectively
enclose a central clearing, and that was the area
the two girls made for as they left the house.

Unnoticed by Katy or Sam, the owl that had
stood guard outside Katy's bedroom the night
before glided silently after them and perched in
the top branches of one of the water elms.   The
bird was white, with no markings at all.   Its black
button eyes glimmered savagely from behind the
white feathers of its round face, and it pressed its
powerful talons deep into the branch.

Katy looked around the little clearing.   A light
snow was beginning to fall.

"Okay.   Dump the bag here," she instructed
Sam.   The shoes made a small heap in the thin

snow. "Now, I guess, just take each pair and put it at the base of one of the trees."

Once that had been done, Katy seemed to hesitate. "Here's where I sort of run out of ideas," she admitted to Sam.

"Do you remember exactly what Lise told you?" Sam asked.

"She said 'call them.' But I don't really know how to do that. Like if maybe there's something special you're supposed to say. I figured Mrs. Pye would tell me..." Katy suppressed an urge to cry. Not only did she miss her friend--more than ever she needed her mentor.

Sam picked up a pair of slippers and held them out to Katy. "So call."

Katy reluctantly took the shoes in her own hands. They were black leather with very long laces, a soft shoe, but of a design she had never seen before. She reached in her mind for their owner, and heard a name echo in her head: *Bonnie.*

Katy heard a gasp from Sam. She looked up and saw Sam's gaze fixed on the lake. Katy followed her stare.

Across the lake a shape was moving through the air, making a sort of empty pocket in the falling snow. It seemed to hesitate at the water's edge, and Katy called again in her mind, *"Bonnie..."* The shape came on.

This emptiness, this formlessness, floated without a sound closer and closer until it stood-- hovered--in front of Katy. There it stopped.

Katy held out the little shoes, and the shape seemed to caress them, to wind itself around them, stroking them as if it had found a cherished and long-lost memento.

Katy received an impression of rich green valleys; music that she recognized as somehow

Celtic; the feet of a hundred people, many of them brothers, sisters, cousins, tall and fair, striking the floor in intricate rhythms, sweat pouring, hearts pounding...

Katy felt, rather than saw, the shape smile sadly. It did not--could not--take the shoes from her, so she set them down gently on the ground at the base of the tree.

The shape slipped the lower edge of itself into them, becoming slightly better defined as it did so. Katy could almost make out Bonnie's face as a negative image where the falling snow encountered her empty but occupied space.

Katy glanced toward Sam, who had paled to almost snow-color herself.

"I... I can see... something..." Sam stammered. Her legs gave out underneath her and she sank down to the ground. "I didn't think... I mean, I never *saw* anything before!"

Katy glared at her sternly. "Don't you dare faint, Samantha Mia! Not here and not now."

"Oh... okay... I won't... Just... just let me sit here a minute, all right? I... Sorry. It was a surprise, that's all," she finished weakly.

Katy moved on to the next pair of shoes, child-sized leather boots decorated with a floral motif. In her hands they spun a sense of cold, mountainous landscape. The patterns of thought they held were alien to Katy, half-oriental, but belonging to a name almost her own: Katya.

The shape that in life had owned that name and those boots flew swiftly across the water and dove eagerly into the shoes.

Nine more times she called. Nine more empty shapes traveled across the lake, some with a rush of purpose, some with shy hesitation, to take their places under the trees before Hugh Langford's house.

Finally the only shoes still unclaimed were Lise Moreau's.

Eleven clear, empty shapes stood like crystal children under the water elms and waited.

Waited, as they had waited for Hugh Langford's summons while their hearts still beat and their eyes still saw and their feet still danced. As they had waited in small lonely rooms, their lives seized, their childhoods stolen, their minds shredded until insanity or death came like a sweet gift.

They had, each of them, loved and trusted one man, one monster, in all their lives: Hugh Langford. Each of them had allowed him to drain them of their life, drop by precious drop, so that he could live on. Because of their love and trust, they had willingly given, allowed, urged it on him. He had taken their lives and discarded these empty shapes.

The eleven stood silent and waiting. They stood while the snow fell and the sun set and the darkness deepened.

They still stood waiting when Hugh Langford's black automobile pulled into the long driveway and came to a stop in front of the house.

Chapter 19:

Judgment

Katy and Sam slipped into the shadows behind the trees, more invisible in the darkness than the ghosts.

Hugh Langford remained sitting behind the wheel, speaking into his cell phone, concluding his instructions to the warehouse manager for storage of the *Nutcracker* sets.

Lise Moreau got out of the car alone. Without explanation to Langford, she walked down to the water elms. Without a glance at Katy or Sam, she took her place in the circle of shapes, picking up the ballet slippers from her lost childhood and facing the eleven.

Above them, at the top of the little rise that led from the lake to the house, Hugh Langford opened his car door and stepped out into the snow. He walked briskly up the steps, stopped at the front door and turned toward where Lise stood under the water elms, a slight frown of irritation on his face.

Lise Moreau slowly turned away from the eleven and looked toward Langford.

Tendrils of twelve awarenesses reached toward him. Separate but linked evidences of twelve long memories were searched. A joined intention, a sigh without breath was released up through the falling snow, pronouncing one word: *"Guilty."*

The wind from their sigh rose through the bare branches of the elms and ruffled the feathers of the white owl watching above them. As if in reply, she spread her huge wings and flapped them noisily, snapping them through the air around her branch.

From its hiding place deep in her feathers, a firefly took flight and circled her head, then returned to its warm refuge. The firefly was rose-colored, and a close examination would have revealed tiny markings etched on its wings like Roman numerals. Only not quite.

Hugh Langford saw only Lise standing alone under the water elms. And she had ceased to concern him. He turned and went into the house.

When Langford disappeared through the front door, Sam turned to Katy and whispered, "Now what?"

Katy didn't exactly have an answer for that, and she felt a little idiotic--as though she had come charging up to the castle screaming a battle cry, and the enemy had simply closed the door and gone in to dinner, leaving her standing on the doorstep with sword drawn and a stupid look on her face.

"I don't know for sure," she said hesitantly, "but somehow I think we need to get him to come down here."

"Maybe I could run up to the house and--I don't know--tell him you're down here hurt or something?"

Katy looked dubious. "No..." she said slowly. "What would you be doing here?"

Lise stood in front of the two girls, in her eyes a look of deadly determination. She replaced her shoes at the base of the twelfth tree and held out her hand commandingly to Katy and nodded her head toward the house. She had long since lost the habit of speech, but her communication was clear: Katy was to come with her to the house.

"I don't think that's such a great idea, Katy," Sam objected. "What if you get in there, and he does his snake charmer thing again, and you just... stay? Then what do I do?"

Katy looked into Lise's eyes. They were clear and intelligent. And angry.

"You have a plan, don't you?" she asked Lise. Lise nodded calmly. "And if his attention is on me, then that frees you to carry it out?" Lise nodded again.

Katy found those cold and merciless eyes reassuring. A hatred that profound was like a heat-seeking missile. "All right then, let's go. Sam, wait here."

Before Sam could object again, Katy took Lise's hand and headed up the little hill toward the house.

Sam was left standing in the clearing, surrounded by eleven ghostly sentinels. She looked around at her dimly visible companions and shuddered.

"Sure," she muttered grimly, addressing the ghosts. "There she goes into the warm house.

'Sam, you wait out here in the snow.   Again!'
Sure, Katy. No problem. At least there aren't any
rats this time. The rats took one look at you guys
and they all dropped dead of heart attacks.   No
offense."

  She stomped her feet in the snow, partly to try
to warm them up, and partly out of sheer helpless
frustration and worry.

Chapter 20:

Ceremony

As Katy and Lise entered the house, they were met in the entryway by Hugh Langford.

"There you are, Katy! I was looking for you. Sorry we were so late, my dear. The strike took longer than I had anticipated. I hope you weren't too bored? It was a poor way to treat my new protégée, leaving her all alone like that. Forgive me?"

His smile reached into the depths of Katy's heart and drew her happily to him. She released Lise's hand and walked to his waiting hug.

"I had a great time! I love antiques, and everything is so beautiful here! I... I explored a little..."

A mental hiccup stopped Katy's happy babble for a moment. Exploring? And wasn't she supposed to do a barre? Why hadn't she?

"I... I just can't believe this is really happening to me," she continued, still puzzling a little, but picking up momentum again. "It's the most exciting thing that ever happened in my whole

life. And I'm going to make you very proud of me,"
she promised.

The delight and gratitude were genuine and
heartfelt.   The eleven spirits, the journals, the
secret rooms with their thirteen pedestals and
three hundred journals, all forgotten in the joy of
being with this wonderful, wonderful man.

"Well then, we'd better get to work, don't you
think? Or do you want some supper first?"

Katy shook her head decisively.   "I'm not
hungry. I'd rather dance. Are you going to give
me a class?"

His smile was secretive but warm, like a
father with a gift hidden behind his back. "Better.
Go and get changed. I'll meet you in the theater
on the second floor. Did you see it when you were
exploring?"

A small frown clouded Katy's face, and she
shuddered slightly, for no reason that she could
understand.   She shook off the feeling and
nodded, a little uncertainly.

"Yes... I--I saw it. It was beautiful. With the
sculptures and the velvet curtains all around."

"Good. I'll meet you there as soon as you
dress.   You, too, Lise," he added as an
afterthought. The secretive smile appeared again
as he asked, "Do you know Albinoni's Adagio,
Katy?"

ح

As Katy quickly slipped into her dance
clothes, she sneaked envious sidelong glances at
the black velvet unitard that Lise pulled over her
slender body. Her own simple leotards and tights
looked laughably childish, like pajamas with feet
in them.

She slipped her shoes on, and something
tugged at her mind... Something about shoes...
She shook her head impatiently.

Lise wrapped herself in her long black velvet cape. Katy gazed at her in frank admiration, but shivered when Lise returned her smile with a cold hard stare.

Don't care if she hates me, Katy decided. *Doesn't matter. She'll be gone soon.* I'm *the new Lise.*

Katy turned and bounced down the stairs, her nose a little higher in the air than was strictly polite.

In the theater, Hugh Langford paced back and forth, his one eye sparkling in anticipation of the evening. As Katy skipped to him, he caught her up like a small child and tossed her lightly into the air, catching her at the last fraction of a second as she dropped laughing into his arms.

"All right," he said sternly, pointing his finger at her in mock reproof. "That's quite enough of that. Now you work. And if I'm not satisfied," he warned ominously, "no supper! Sometimes my students have gone for weeks--months!--without eating until I decide that their arabesque is acceptable."

Katy ducked her head and curtseyed, her eyes wide in playfully pretended fear. "Yes, sir."

"Now go and warm up. Because it is so late, we will start with a bit of choreography. Tomorrow morning we will do a class, but tonight I cannot wait. I must see how my Katy will look in my dances." There was a hungry, canine gleam in his expression.

Katy took the big candelabra he handed her and went to a back corner of the little auditorium where a small barre and a mirror made a tiny one-girl studio space. She stretched out quickly with the abbreviated sequence of barre exercises that she used when she had to warm up in a hurry.

In ten minutes, Hugh Langford came over to her carrying a small bundle wrapped in tissue paper which he handed to Katy almost shyly.

"This is for you. I suppose it's silly to ask you to wear it for a first rehearsal, but I want to see you in it. Do you mind?"

She unwrapped the bundle. Inside was a replica of Lise's black velvet unitard and cape, but in the palest imaginable shade of ivory. The long vertical lines of trim were done in pearls, and there was a pearl collar that would accent Katy's long neck.

It was so beautiful that the sight of it left her a little breathless. She pulled the unitard on over her leotard, carefully, almost reverentially.

"Here," Langford said, holding out the cape, just to get an idea... " And he wrapped the long velvet cloak around her shoulders, throwing one end across to make a deep, graceful sweep of ivory under her chin.

He led her to the mirror, turning her to face her pale, velvet-swathed image, placing the candelabra on a small table beside her so that its light glowed across the pale velvet and warmed the color of her skin.

"Ah, Katy," he sighed. "You are a vision. Take your hair down please, the color is perfect--the ivory with the gold."

She unpinned her hair and shook out her long honey-colored waves over her shoulders. Langford held up the pearl collar, and she lifted her hair for him to fasten it around her neck.

She agreed. She was a vision.

They stood like that a long time staring into the mirror, Langford behind her with his hands on her shoulders. Quietly, almost to himself, he began to speak.

"Everything that I have done in my life, everything that was good, everything that was evil, I have done for the sake of only one passion: beauty.

"Often I have created it. When I could not create it, I bought it or stole it. Even destroyed for it.

"I confess this to you, because what I ask from you, you must give to me freely or not at all. Yours is the choice.

"I have done much that was evil. Truly evil. My life has been longer than you can imagine. Many times I have thought my life *too* long, too difficult, too... costly.

"But while there is beauty such as yours in the world, I cannot leave it. I cannot allow myself to die with such wonders unseen, unappreciated... unpossessed."

He smiled sadly at her in the mirror, then turned her to face him, searching her eyes. "For your sake, Katy, I must stay alive. You can--you *must*--keep me alive. Will you do this?"

He was asking for her oath. Katy knew it. No bride, no nun, no questing knight had ever sworn a vow more binding. If she, like the twelve before her, made this promise, she would never break it. From that whispered syllable forward, she would be his without hope of escape.

Once her promise was made, Hugh Langford's ritual would be done. There would remain only the slow, patient devouring of the human sacrifice. He would linger over this feast--perhaps fifteen or even twenty years of savoring mouthful by mouthful her youth and beauty and strength.

For the first five or so years her mind would writhe and scream, like an animal in a cruel trap. He understood well how to manage them those first five quick years. It was delicate work, tricky. The most taxing for him.

But they were also at their most delicious then--so very beautiful, so full of the electricity of life.

They were tamer after that, after he had drained off some of that powerful current, but also less satisfying--every year a little less until, like Lise Moreau, there was nothing left to take from them.

How he relished the prospect of these next five years with this beauty. And, thanks to Pye, he had begun to suspect that there was more to this one. Much more. Perhaps after this one, he himself would be much more as well...

He would understand better after tonight, after she had danced for him and he had taken his first taste of her.

"Well, my Katy," he asked tenderly, "will you?"

"Yes," she whispered.

The ceremony was done.

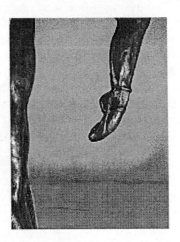

Chapter 21:

The First Lesson

He smiled down at her fondly, and she smiled back. "Enough dress-up," he teased. "First you must learn my dance. You may have the cape back when there is less danger that you will trip on it."

Katy laughed and reluctantly removed the cape. She hugged it once to herself, then exchanged it for the inexpensive rehearsal cape he offered her and headed for the stage.

Lise stood center-stage, wrapped in her black cape. Katy looked to Langford for instructions, and he motioned her up onto the stage as well.

"Lise will dance this through for you, Katy," he told her. "Learn the choreography as quickly as you can. We'll probably work quite late tonight. I want to see you dance at least the first section before we stop."

She nodded her agreement and took up the understudy's position at the back of the stage.

Lise began dancing, while Katy marked the steps behind, struggling to follow without verbal instructions.

Repetition followed repetition while Langford prowled and paced along the front edge of the stage, watching Katy's movements with a predatory intensity. Often he called impatient corrections to her. More than once he leapt onto the stage to push or pull her physically when she misinterpreted Lise's movements.

Very quickly, riding her feeling of inspiration and and confidence, Katy memorized the opening sequence. Within twenty or thirty minutes, she began to understand the structure of the short section. It involved complicated work with the long cape, but the steps themselves were simple. Elegant, beautiful, but really quite simple.

After building the chain of movements, Langford let the two dancers try the sequence through once with the music. He interrupted them with a scream.

"*No!!!*" he shouted. "Can't you hear? Can't you see? You dance like a cow! That is *not* what she showed you!"

Katy stepped back in shock. Teachers had raised their voices to her before, but not like this. He hurled words at her viciously, like thrown knives. He wanted to wound and humiliate her. He *wanted* it. He was *enjoying* it. Instantly, tears sprang to her eyes.

Langford continued his tirade, shaking an angry finger at her to punctuate his words. "When you are *told* what to do, when you are *shown* what to do, that is what you are *expected* to do. This is not your little studio where you can behave like a spoiled child. I'm warning you: do the step--*my* step, not your own--and do it correctly. Or get off my stage." And he turned his back on her and stalked off.

With an effort, Katy gathered herself together and tried it again.

"Better," he called from the back of the theater where he now stood. "Not good. But better. Do it again. Higher legs. Longer balance."

She did it again. And again. Six times. Ten. She was sweating and gasping for air. The eleventh time she fell, twisting her ankle.

Langford reached onto the stage and grabbed her arm. She hid her face and shrank back, afraid that he might hit her.

"Katy? Are you all right?" There was only tenderness and concern in his voice. She looked up and the love in his eyes, after his terrifying fury, made her burst into tears.

"I'm... I'm so so-or-ory..." she sobbed. She scrambled to her feet, pushing the tears away roughly with both hands. "I... I'll do it again..."

She started to hobble back to her place, ducking her head to hide her shame.

Instantly he was beside her, his arm around her, soothing her with the sound of his voice.

"No. It's enough. It's enough, Katy. Come and have a rest. It's my fault. I am pushing you too hard. Too fast. Come and sit for a moment. Have a drink of water."

He led her to the single chair and seated her there. In a moment he reappeared with a glass of cool water which she drank down in one long swallow.

"Is your ankle all right?" Katy nodded. "While you rest," he said quietly, "you will watch Lise do this. You will sit and rest and learn."

He motioned to Lise, who re-wrapped her cape around herself and returned silently to the center

of the stage.   The candle flames threw gold
reflections into her dark green eyes.   Those eyes
glittered now with purpose.

Langford re-started the music and crouched
down beside Katy where she sat in his chair. Katy
was trying desperately to absorb every nuance of
Lise's movements as the dark-haired dancer
began the slow sweeping circles with her cape.

Katy watched Lise; Langford watched Katy.
His one eye never wandered from her face.

"You see how it goes, Katy?" he whispered
throatily. "Watch her. You must learn quickly,
Katy. We cannot truly begin until you master the
dance. I must see you dance it. Now. Tonight."

Lise sank to her knees now, billowing the
cape behind her and then contracting and rising
as she circled it: overhead, along the floor,
overhead, along the floor.

The footlight flames danced wildly from the
displaced air.

Langford's breath was hot in her ear as Katy
struggled to concentrate on Lise's movements.

"Dance for me, Katy. Now. Dance the steps
that I gave you. Let me watch you."

Lise's cape swung wide, hypnotic in its
patterns, swinging over the flames of the
footlights, arcing up to the   chandeliers.

Langford's voice trembled with urgency and
need.   "You promised me, my Katy.   You
promised. To feed me with your beauty. To keep
me alive. With your strength and your youth."

Katy's eyes began to register understanding.
That was it! That movement there. She saw what
she had done wrong. Now she could do it...

She slowly rose from the chair, moving toward
the stage, hardly noticing as Langford pulled the
rehearsal cape away from her and, with hands

that shook slightly, placed the heavy velvet one about her shoulders.

Now she could dance it, she was sure. Now she could give him what he needed from her... What she had promised...

As the velvet cape was laid onto Katy's slender shoulders, Lise Moreau lifted her head, feeling the bonds that had chained her mind and body for so many years loosen and drop from her. She stared directly into Katy's eyes. And smiled. At the same instant she slowly--too slowly--dragged her black cloak across the footlight candles.

A corner of it caught fire.

Chapter 22:

The Betrayed

Still smiling, Lise swung the other corner of the cape up to the chandelier, where it, too, ignited.

Hugh Langford leapt to his feet, grabbed Katy's arm, and pulled her toward him. Katy could not take her eyes off Lise.

The music still played, Lise still danced with perfect, heart-rending grace. But she was surrounded now by flames that she carefully spread from her cape to the stage draperies. She was laughing, playing with the flames as though they were the skirts of her costume, floating them about her until the entire stage was engulfed.

Langford slowly backed away from the stage and the spreading flames until Lise leapt lightly to the floor, running toward him and dragging her

flaming cape to set the rug afire. He turned and
fled, pulling Katy with him.

In Katy's last glance backward she saw Lise
laughing and circling the theater, fire from her
cape licking at each section of drapery she
passed. She met Katy's eyes and leapt back up
onto the burning stage where she threw both ends
of fiery fabric above her head like wings--another
flaming angel.

Hugh Langford dragged Katy onto the second-
floor landing, where she struggled with him,
fighting to get back to Lise as smoke and flame
came billowing out of the theater door.

Langford picked Katy up in his arms and ran
down the stairs as the fire caught the old
carpeting and raced after them, chasing them
down and toward the front door.

Langford stopped at the base of the stairs to
put Katy down and push her toward the front
door just as Sam ran up the driveway screaming
her name.

Sam grabbed Katy's arm; Langford grabbed
one of the bronze sculptures from its marble base
and wrestled it out the door. It was the only thing
he had time to save before the fire found the gas
line.

The shock of the explosion sent Katy and Sam
flying across the driveway, knocking the breath
out of them as they landed. Katy was conscious
of burning debris falling around her, then of
scrambling to her feet.

She saw Langford, limping as he cradled the
bronze dancer with one arm, his other arm
dangling by his side uselessly, broken when the
explosion had hurled him down. Ignoring Sam,
who staggered down toward the clearing, Katy ran
to his side.

The heat from the blazing house was so intense that it forced them back further into the trees.   Langford gasped out that the car might explode, and they moved back further still.

Then Katy was helping him to the ground, calling his name and trying to gently wipe the blood from his face where it had been cut by shards of flying window.   She was bleeding, too, and the ivory velvet of her unitard was soon streaked with their mingled blood.

The horrifying beauty and power of the fire held them transfixed, neither of them conscious that they had now backed into the little clearing in the trees.   Or that they were not alone.

Katy heard it first.   A sigh going up like a breath.   A single word.

"Guilty."

She looked around her and saw empty shapes like crystal children.   As she watched, the eleven shapes became twelve.   Inside the burning house, Langford's twelfth victim had died, and a new transparent form materialized above Lise Moreau's shoes.

A moment later, Langford saw them, too.   His one eye narrowed in wary cunning.

He dropped the bronze sculpture, and with his uninjured hand, gripped Katy's arm, pulling himself to his feet.   His fingers cut painfully into her flesh, but she did not protest.

Sam approached Katy, calling her name softly.

Katy did not reply.   Her whole concern was fixed on Langford.   His was fixed on the Twelve.

"Guilty..." came the sigh.

"Who are you?"   Langford demanded of the shapes.

"We are your children.   We are the Twelve," came the whisper.

"I have no children. The Twelve are dead."
Langford seemed unafraid, scornful.

Katy was less so. Sam called her again, and
this time Katy looked at her, frowning slightly,
trying to remember, to understand.

"We are the Twelve," the whisper repeated.
"We are the children who loved you."

"What do you want?"

"Betrayer..." came the whisper. *"Give us
back..."*

"I have nothing of yours," Langford declared
flatly. He tried to limp out of the circle, pulling
Katy. The shapes did not move, but he could not
pass. Something blocked his way.

Katy heard a complex sound begin to build, a
sound like breath under a sound like a heartbeat.

Sam reached out slowly and took Katy's free
hand. Katy winced, her mind pulled in two
opposing directions.

The whisper divided itself now into twelve
separate voices, each calling softly, *"I claim what
is mine..."*

Katy thought the heartbeat increased slightly
in its rhythm and strength.

"You gave me!" Langford shouted angrily.
"Freely! You swore an oath to me!"

"I claim what is mine... Betrayer... "

"No! I deny it! It is you who betrayed me!
You who failed *me!*"

The implacable reply came, *"Betrayer... I
claim what is mine..."*

Now Katy was sure. The heart was beating
much faster.

A sound came from Langford's throat which
was half a choke, half a scream. Katy looked up
into his face and saw the patch begin to bulge
outward. He released his hold on her arm to grab

at it, trying to hold into himself the life that was pushing outward. The muscles in his arm shook violently with the effort.

Sam gathered Katy into her arms, calling her name over and over, watching her still-dilated pupils for a sign of recognition. Katy allowed herself to be held, but would not move further from Langford.

From between Langford's fingers, a vaporous fog oozed outward, cold and thick. Slowly, inexorably, it pushed the patch and his hand away from his face until the band that held the patch in place snapped. Langford fell to the ground, screaming in pain and fury as the fog rushed out of him, covering his body.

The sound of the breath and the heartbeat resonated through the woods now. Still Sam spoke gently, lovingly in Katy's ear, calling her back, reminding her.

Katy started to remember.

From the emptiness behind Hugh Langford's face came twelve gelatinous masses, one by one crawling through the fog, over his contorted body. Slowly, laboriously they arranged their ectoplasmic bodies into the shape of lovely graceful children.

One by one, they floated, smiling, holding out soft, welcoming arms, toward the empty, crystal-like forms under the trees. One by one. Filling, uniting.

Above the Twelve, filling the branches of the leafless water elms and extending to the horizon and beyond in all directions, a Presence gathered. A vast and welcoming Consciousness.

As each of the twelve shapes filled, there came from the Presence a soft welcoming *"ahhhhh..."*, like a thousand soft exhalations, filled with joy and grief, loss and unhoped-for redemption.

The Twelve, one by one, lifted into the falling snow, floating silently upward.

An opening--a doorway--formed, folding back tree limbs, then clouds, then stars.

The Twelve floated upward; their outlines were barely visible, like soap bubbles. They danced as they floated toward the Entity, weightless and effortless. They moved as all dancers move in their minds, with perfect control, with absolute freedom, suspended in space and time, beyond gravity or muscle-and-bone.

From the Consciousness above her, a sensation of warmth and gratitude flowed across Katy's face and through her heart. If she could have, Katy would have climbed that marvelous touch into the enfolding Presence.

It left her slowly, like the gentle withdrawing of a lingering kiss. As Pye had promised her, a door had opened and she had met the Power behind it face to face.

As the last of the Twelve were enfolded, the door closed gently behind her, and the Presence was gone.

Chapter 23:

My Katy

Katy, still held tightly in Sam's arms, looked down at the now-still form of Hugh Langford on the ground. She remembered now. Sam had called her back.

"It's okay," she assured Sam. "I'm okay. Thank you."

Sam squinted at her. "What?"

"It's okay. I'm fine. You can let me go."

"*What?*"

"Can't you hear me?" Katy wriggled an arm free and pointed to her ear.

"I can't hear you," Sam shouted. "I have plugs in my ears. Has the sound stopped?"

"What?" Katy asked, puzzled. This was starting to sound like a vaudeville routine.

"If the weird sound has stopped," Sam yelled, "nod your head."

Katy did, and Sam pulled the wax plugs out of her ears, holding them up with a self-satisfied smile. "I sound-proofed myself. So I wouldn't zone out." Sam looked over at the motionless form of Hugh Langford. "Do you think he's dead?" she asked nervously.

"I guess we should check," Katy said hesitantly. Something in him still pulled at her heart, and before Sam could stop her, she knelt down and put a soft hand on his chest.

Instantly the muffled timpani sound of the heartbeat reverberated through her body. Langford's eyelid snapped open, and a smile played around the edges of his mouth.

Behind them Sam stiffened, and her face went blank.

"Katy..." he whispered, his voice coiling itself around her mind once again, burrowing in. His unbroken arm slid onto the small of her back. "My Katy... You've come to me, haven't you? You've come to save me. As you promised. Haven't you?"

"Yes," she whispered.

"They've hurt me, Katy."

"I know."

"They tried to kill me." Katy wept at his pain. "But you came to save me. Save me, my Katy, my beautiful Katy. Come into me. As you promised. Do it now. Dance for me. Save me."

Katy knew what he needed. She understood. She began to hum softly, moving her arms like wings spreading over him, dancing for him where she knelt.

"Katy..." he whispered, "Save me..."

She looked down into the gaping hole in his face. It was a vast, magical cavern. Once inside she would not only dance--she would *fly*! They would fly together, forever young and strong and achingly beautiful!

Katy swept her arms back, arching from the base of her spine. She understood, not with her mind, but with her body, how her physical self could impel her life force into him, saving him, giving her life for his.

She was ready. One perfect, beautiful movement...

A blur of white fury hit the diminishing gap between Katy and Langford. White wings beat backward into Katy's face, driving her back. Savage talons gripped the edge of that vast beckoning emptiness, piercing the flesh and bone that rimmed it.

Hugh Langford screamed in agony as the white owl struck him. He rolled away, beating at the bird.

Katy was flung backward into the unseeing Sam, who fell to the ground and lay there quietly.

Katy untangled herself from Sam and scrambled on her hands and knees to make a desperate grab for the owl.

She dug her fingers into the bird's body below the wings at the top of the legs, and pulled. The owl screeched with pain and rage but did not release her hold on Langford's face.

Katy squeezed harder, forcing the bird to turn its attention to her counter-attack. She struck at Katy's hands with her beak now, forcing Katy to let go, but Katy grabbed again above the wings,

her fingers working deep into the feathers around
the owl's neck.

Katy's fingers tightened down. As she gripped
harder and harder, the bird slowly released her
talons, and Langford rolled away, still screaming
and holding his face.

But Katy didn't stop--*wouldn't* stop until the
bird was dead.

Across the snow, a yowling projectile of fur
and teeth and claws hit Katy square in the back,
knocking her onto her face and leaving her
gasping for breath.

Nijinska had traveled fast and long over rough
ground; her wounded, bleeding paws left small
crimson imprints on Katy's back.

The owl dropped to the ground, momentarily
stunned. The cat approached the bird cautiously.
She gently nudged at the white neck feathers with
her nose, then, claws carefully retracted, with her
paw.

The owl stirred. With an abrupt flurry of
wings and tail, she fluttered to her feet.

Katy recovered her breath as the two
predators divided on either side of their quarry.
The owl glided to a branch on Langford's left,
wings held wide, head low. Nijinska slunk in a
deep crouch to his right; the fur at her neck stood
up like the ruff of a lion, and a low screeching
growl came from far inside her chest.

Langford had risen to his feet and was slowly
backing away from the animals toward the lake,
holding his face, blood running through his
fingers.

"Katy!" he called hoarsely, beseechingly.

Katy looked quickly from owl to cat, trying to
decide which was the greater danger to him,
which one she should attack.

With a quick, sharp rotation of its head, the owl shifted its stare from the man to the girl, seeming to consider the events to come.

From out of the white feathers, like the sparks that still flew upward from the burning house, came an uncountable swarm of fireflies--hundreds, thousands of fireflies.

They filled every inch of the air around Katy. The light they cast into her eyes was blinding. Every time she tried to beat through them or turn away, they regrouped, encasing her in a moving cylinder of light, screening her from the sight of the hunt taking place in front of her.

But despite the fanning sound of thousands of minute beating wings, Katy could hear. She heard Nijinska's yowl escalate to a wild battle cry. She heard the owl join its own shriek to the cat's. She heard Langford running, screaming as he ran. The sound of the owl's wings followed him through the trees, down the slope, toward the lake.

Through the thousand fireflies, Katy could see nothing of what happened by the water. All she knew was the retreating sound of the heartbeat, the sudden cessation of the screams of the animals and the man, a long frantic of sound of water splashing.

And then silence. A silence absolute except for the continued crackling and popping of the burning house behind her.

The fireflies left her as quickly as they had come. They filled the tree branches above the clearing like Christmas lights, twinkling slowly, almost meditatively.

Katy stood sobbing; her heart felt torn and bleeding from the whipsaw of her encounters with Langford.

Behind her, Sam blinked and shook her head, then came to her friend's side where they clung to each other, both crying now, and beginning to shiver from cold and fear.

Sam took off her coat and wrapped it around Katy, who had lost her cape and wore only the thin unitard in which she had fled the fire.

The white owl glided silently toward them from the lake, skimming low to the ground on her wide wings, barely visible against the snow.

Beneath her trotted Nijinska, soaking wet and limping a bit on her tattered paws, looking more rodent than feline.

As Nijinska ran to be caught up in Katy's arms, the owl swooped upward into a water elm. She perched on the lowest branch of the tree, and the fireflies slowly adjusted their position around her, bathing her with gentle lights. The owl stretched out her wings and beat the air around her with a series of quick flurries. The movement sent the smell of nutmeg drifting down into Katy's upturned face.

Katy heard in her memory's ear a soft grandmotherly voice saying, *"Who you are, Katy Moon--what you are--is not hidden from me."*

Katy lifted one hand to the owl in greeting and spoke quietly through her tears, "I see you, Pye. And I *know* you. Thank you."

The owl blinked her fierce dark eyes in acknowledgment.

In the distance, Sam heard the first faint sirens of fire trucks, and she gently led Katy toward the road.

Epilogue:

Christmas Eve With Family

Christmas Eve found Katy in her own bed, her cuts and scrapes and one minor burn bandaged carefully. Nijinska lay asleep beside her in a furry circle on her pillow, one still-tender paw tangled in Katy's hair for reassurance.

Following the fire, there had been some gentle questions from the police, neatly ducked with her completely plausible explanation of loss of consciousness following the explosion.

The deaths of Hugh Langford and Lise Moreau had been hesitantly explained to her, with no elaborating details, by her father.   She had already known more than he told her, but the mention of their names brought a healing opportunity to weep in her father's arms.

She had talked to Sam by phone every couple of hours. Sam was officially grounded for her fib about the "slumber party," but the girls had convinced both sets of parents to let them meet Christmas evening after supper to exchange gifts and compare their Santa loot.

Everyone felt without saying so that it would be a start at re-normalizing their lives with a little uncomplicated Christmas greed.

Now Katy lay in the dark, relishing the warmth of her cat, and looking out where the full moon shone into the branches of the tree next to

her window. A soft knock came on her bedroom
door, and her father's head peeked around the
edge of the door.

"Elf?" he whispered. "You asleep?"

"No, Daddy," she said, scooting to a sitting
position cautiously so as not to wake Nijinska.
"Come on in." She put up a warning hand. "But
not too fast. Look out my window."

Michael Moon tiptoed to the bed and sat down
carefully, letting out a long low whistle of
surprise. "Wow! Katy, do you know what that is?
That's a Snowy Owl!"

Katy smiled. "Really?"

"I've only seen one once before--and certainly
not this far south. They summer up in the Arctic
Circle, and they only come down into Canada and
the northern U.S. in the winter. If we look
carefully, we'll see some dark markings in his coat
like speckles."

"*Her* coat," corrected Katy. "And she doesn't
have any speckles. She's pure white."

"We probably just can't see them," said her
father, peering intently through the glass. "The
young ones all have dark markings, and by the
time their coats turn pure white, they never leave
the Arctic. But I sure don't *see* any markings."

"No markings, Daddy. None at all."

They sat together on the bed for a long time,
holding hands and watching the stately bird as
she sat like a guardian ghost outside Katy's room.

Tomorrow, Katy thought, she would hang the
pair of colorful toe-socks in the tree; they would
make a warm nest.

Michael broke the silence by clearing his
throat and pulling out of his pocket a *Nutcracker*
program and his pen. "I wonder if you would mind
autographing this for me?"

Katy laughed. "Sorry, sir. I already signed one for you. My agent..."

"I know, Miss Moon," he said quickly, "but that was only for Clara. I thought you were much more interesting in 'Snow.'"

Katy's breath caught in her throat. "Did you come?"

"Believe it or not, I did. Last night. Know what I saw?" Katy shook her head, afraid to speak. "Absolute elegance."

He tried to say more but couldn't quite get the words out. There were tears standing in his eyes that matched the ones in hers.

He gruffly produced a small, clumsily wrapped present which he poked into her hands.

"Ummm... I wanted to give this to you before the mad scramble tomorrow morning," he mumbled. "Sorry about the wrapping."

Rebecca Moon insisted on doing all the gift-wrapping for the household herself because she liked things to be color-coordinated under the tree. None of the rest of the family had much opportunity to practice, and they were all maladept with paper and ribbon.

Katy hugged him hard. "Thanks, Daddy."

"It's nothing very much. Just sort of family memorabilia. Probably not worth a hug. You know, when it comes to presents, I'm not a very good picker."

Katy was not a careful paper-opener. She ripped into the present like a starving man into a steak. It was an old photograph, inexpensively framed. She couldn't see it well, so she reached for the light.

"It's my grandmother," her father said. "The one I told you about. With the eyebrows like ours. That book she's holding was one of her 'Magic Books.'"

Katy looked down at the photograph. An adorable little old lady with a round face and messy white braids stared back at her, her eyes laughing behind her little gold-rimmed round glasses. She was wearing a ridiculous dress of silk patches, and the book she held had markings on the cover like Roman numerals. Only not quite.

It was a black-and-white photograph, but Katy knew that the book was rose-colored.

"Her name was Maggie?" Katy frowned, understanding and not understanding. "Maggie Moon?"

Michael chuckled, "Well, that's what my mother insisted people call Gramma Moon. She was christened 'Magpie,' but that was way too hillbilly for my mother."

"Thank you so much, Daddy." Katy kissed his ear with special tenderness.

She was beginning to see her father more clearly, this loving and gifted man whose greatest possibility in life had slipped away from him. It added a fierce protectiveness to her love for him.

"You picked great."

Michael's gaze drifted back to the white owl, still sitting patiently in the cold moonlight. "If your owl stays, you'll have to name her."

"Pye," Katy murmured absently, smiling up from the photograph of her great-grandmother. "Her name is Pye, Daddy. And she's not going anywhere. She's going to introduce me to some people. When I'm ready."

ೋ

For information about the second book of
The Katy Moon Chronicles: The Game,
visit www.katymoon.com.

About
the Author

Julie   Lambert
has   been   a
dance   teacher
and   choreogra-
pher   for   over
twenty years, in-
cluding thirteen years as Artistic Director for a
professional   dance   company   in   Dallas.   Ms.
Lambert now lives in Montréal where she works
as a sculptor and writer and collaborates with her
husband, choreographer Gilles Tanguay, on dance
projects. Her dance theater works have been
performed for over a quarter of a million people
and are currently in performance in both French
and English.

The Sculptures:

Bronze   dance
sculptures by Ms.
Lambert, including those featured in the Katy
Moon books, are available for purchase. Each
piece is limited to eight numbered castings and
two Artist Proofs.

For details, please visit her website at
www.katymoon.com

Glossary

This is in no way meant to be a technical dictionary of dance and theatrical terms--just a few brief notes to help out non-dancer readers. If you have further questions about dance, I invite you to visit our website at katymoon.com.

Adagio - a slow dance section (or piece of music)

Arabesque - a position standing on one leg with the other leg extended behind

Balancé - a waltz-like triple step

Bourrée- a series of tiny foot movements on pointe that move across the floor almost as if you were floating

Dégagé - extending one foot with the knee straight, the toe pointed, and with the foot brushed slightly off the ground

Échappé - a movement from 5th position to 2nd either by sliding the feet or jumping

Grand Allegro - a series of dance steps with big jumps

Grand Battement - like a dégagé, but brushed very high

Half pointe or demi-pointe - on the ball of the foot with the heel lifted as high as possible.

Pas de Bourrée - a triple step in a pattern such as back, side, front

Pas de deux - a dance for two people, usually a male and a female

Passé - standing on one foot, the other foot lifted until the toe touches the knee

Petit Allegro - a quick series of dance steps with rapid foot movements and small jumps

Pirouette - a turn done on one leg

Places - the area in the wings from where the performers make their entrance

Plié - bending the knee(s) that you're standing on, can be **demi** (small) or **grand** (large)

Pointe or full pointe - on the ends of the toes.

Pointe shoes - special shoes that make it possible to dance on pointe.

Port de Bras - movements of the arms

Positions of the feet

1st - heels together, toes pointing out

2nd - like 1st, but with heels about 12 inches apart

5th - one foot in front of the other, toes outward, the heel of each foot touching the toe of the other

4th - feet parallel like 5th, but with one foot several inches in front of the other

B+ - on one foot, the other knee bent, foot pointed and resting on the floor behind

Relevé - rising from a flat foot to pointe or demi-pointe

Révérénce - a combination of bows and curtseys that usually closes a ballet class

Sous-sus - from 5th position, relevé with the legs pulled tightly together

Spot - a snap of the head while turning (keeps you from getting dizzy)

Stage manager - the person in charge backstage during the actual performance

Stage Right - to the performer's right as she faces the audience

Sugar Plum, Giselle, Odette - the staring roles for ballerinas in *Nutcracker, Giselle,* and *Swan Lake.*

Tendu - like a dégagé but with the extended toe touching the ground

Turnout - rotating the legs from the hip socket so that the toes point outward, critical for achieving a correct classical "look"

Tutu - a traditional ballet costume with short or long skirts of net or tulle

Wings - the areas on the sides of the stage that are hidden from the audience